THE BOYS OF BIG RUG

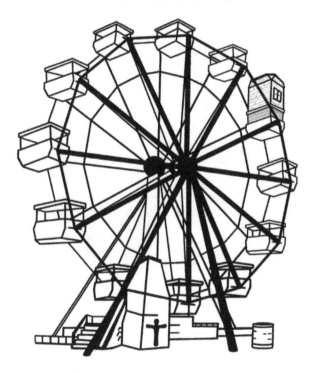

T.J. MORGAN

Green Lemon
PUBLISHING

For permission requests, contact T.J. Morgan and/or
Green Lemon Publishing at tjmorganbooks@gmail.com

Book Cover & Illustrations by T.J. Morgan of Green Lemon Publishing.
Formatting & Design by T.J. Morgan & Whitney Morgan of Green Lemon Publishing.
Creative Director, Whitney Morgan of Green Lemon Publishing.

For more by T.J. Morgan, please visit TJMorganBooks on Instagram.

ISBN 978-1-964102-01-6
First printing 2024

Thank you for reading.

Enjoy...

CONTENTS

———

Foreword by Jerry BoJon, GED

FOREWORD

———

As an oil man, and proud employee of Fast Lube Express, I read words almost every day. I've also read several books from start to finish.

The Boys of Big Rug, previously known as *Tuck's Memoirs,* and originally titled *Tuck's Regional History Project for 11ᵗʰ Grade Extra Credit,* is a warm-hearted tale of boys being boys.

Teetering back and forth between ridiculous and insightful, you'll find yourself smiling with every page. Transport yourself back to where you're going, to a simpler time filled with complexity. Enjoy getting to know, *The Boys of Big Rug.*

— Jerry BoJon, GED

THE BOYS OF BIG RUG

Tell me something new,
and I'll hear it for the first time.

— *Yoderian proverb*

NAME'S TUCK

My Uncle Shty dropped outta school in the seventh grade to focus on lawnmower repair. He worked, and lived, in the detached garage of a triple-wide trailer owned by a redneck named Cornbread.

"Here's a little secret for ya, Tuck," Uncle Shty confided. "If you live where you work, you're always on time."

Every day, as sure as the sun came up, Uncle Shty, Cornbread, and typically Coach, would be in that garage tinkering with mowers.

"Can't buy this quality," Uncle Shty told me. "It's the personal touch that makes all the difference. I tighten everything by hand. No tools! That-a-way I can feel how tight stuff is. Them tools are expensive too. I ain't rich," his voice raised while tightening a mower blade. "Personal touch is key. I'll tell you this Tuck, when folks bring me a mower, they never come back. Not never have I had a repeat customer… That's how *I know* I'm fixing 'em right."

Coach put his hands on his hips and interjected.

"Big city got personal touch. Had a gal in the city offer me a personal touch for my shoes," he rambled while lifting the heel of his dirty white shoes. "Said no way! These multi-sport sneakers. Can't get these sneakers round here. These big city sneakers!"

Coach has been the Big Rug K–12 gym teacher for as long as I can remember. Not because he's athletically gifted, or knows anything about teaching children, but because his first name is Coach. Principal Keck thought it just made sense.

My mother grew up with Coach. She was his babysitter, even though Coach was a few years older. Mama said Coach was "slow to develop but fast to look funny."

He's thick in the torso, with tiny hips and little short legs—like a cinderblock sittin' on toothpicks. And apparently the good Lord made his head so big that there wasn't room for a neck. Just a head sitting on shoulders. His buzzed blond hair makes his head look flat on top, which really adds to his odd appearance.

One time, Dale, snuck a little folded-up piece of paper on Coach's head, and it was still there the next morning. Dale later confessed he'd put jelly on the paper to make it stick. But still, it stayed on all night without Coach noticing, that's impressive!

And, Coach has the hairiest inner thighs of any man I've ever seen. I'm half certain he combs his inner thigh hair. I know he puts gel in it. Seems like combing it is a reasonable assumption to make.

When I was a kid, Coach wore fancy shorts called boxer briefs. It might as well have been his uniform... Every day, the man wore his white multi-sport sneakers with a baby-blue polo shirt tucked into his boxer briefs and a plastic whistle dangling from his neck.

Mama and I ran into Coach the first time he wore his fancy new shorts around town.

"Picked up ten boxes in the city," Coach told us as his inner thigh hair glistened with hair gel in the sunlight.

"Are you sure they're not undies?" Mama's voice softened as if speaking to a child.

"Box says, boxer brief shorts!" Coach grunted. "It's big city stuff, babe! Big Rug ain't got these... Not even Plumpstin City got these. Besides, these here boxer shorts can't be undies. I'm *wearing* undies. See 'em right here?"

"Yes, Coach," Mama observed, struggling to suppress her laughter. "I can see you're wearing undies."

The outline of Coach's tighty-whities was always visible through his fancy boxer brief shorts.

"Coach...honey...they're just so tight."

"That's how they s'pposed to be," he insisted. "My shirts tucked in...got a belt on...wearin' undies...that means they shorts! Box say *shorts!* Tag say *shorts!* Waistband say *shorts!* It's big city stuff, babe!"

Coach spun his cubed body around and walked off, chewing his gum louder with every step.

"Dismissed!" he shouted and chirped his whistle.

Even today, Coach is a man who takes pride in his clothing. Nowadays he wears those disposable white jumpsuits that painters dress in.

"Wear it for a month, throw it away," he told me. "Never have to wash nothin'."

But rumor has it, Coach still wears his fancy big city boxer brief shorts underneath.

When we were kids, the boys and I would stop by Cornbread's garage on our way home from school to see what kinda mowers Uncle Shty was working on, and look at a few old spark plugs for Brant's jewelry business.

"The smaller ones are better, right?" Dale asked Brant as they rummaged through a box.

"Yawp," Brant said while tying back his knotted locks of black hair with a rubber band. "Lighter sparkplugs don't stretch the earlobes as much."

"Ouch," Ronny cried out. "I sat on a dang gear spoke."

Mitch laughed, "Captain Klutz at it again."

"How'd you think of sparkplug earrings anyway, Brant?" I complained, shifting through junk in a wet cardboard box. "And why the heck is this box all wet?"

"Spittin' in it," Coach hollered from the back of the garage.

I kicked the soggy box away in disgust.

"Ain't spittin' on the floor," Coach scowled. "Who spittin' on the floor? I ain't no goat gobbler... Get civilized... Dismissed!" He grunted and chirped his whistle.

"Got the idea from the pinky-pointer workin' the register at Stuff & Stuff's Nice Things," Brant interrupted Coach to answer my question. "Great guy. And pinky-pointers know fashion!"

Brant would pay Uncle Shty one cent for five dead spark plugs, clean them, spray-paint them, and use them as accent pieces for earrings. The high gloss spray-paint was just gorgeous... Really made the jewelry pop. I'd take one of Brant's spray-painted spark plug earrings over a fancy schmancy diamond any day of the week!

My mother loved them too! The weight of the spark plugs stretched out her earlobes pretty bad. But, like Mama always said, "That's the price you pay for fashion!"

Back in the day, Brant stopped by Uncle Shty's shop every Tuesday to scour through spark plugs. And once he learned how to ride his saddle-dog, YoUber, he went twice a week.

His folks bought the saddle-dog from some Highgrass fancy Dutch traditionalist living down in Chigger Bottom. While Brant's family was being shown the puppies, the breeder's Yoderian accent made it difficult to understand exactly what he was saying.

"Fey yit's yo uber… 'n, fey yit's yo uber… 'n, fey yit's yo uber," the breeder spoke as he pointed at each pup.

Brant's father mistakenly thought the man was saying that all their names were "YoUber."

"This one's YoUber…and, this one's YoUber…"

Brant's saddle-dog was a jerk if you ask me! YoUber always peed on my clothes when we went swimming down at Lake Sippo. And that dang dog was doing it on purpose… I know it!

While Brant foraged through old spark plugs, the rest of us boys would listen to Cornbread share a story or two. He was the best story teller in town, hands down!

Cornbread's real name was Webber York. He got his nickname because of his speech impediment. Uncle Shty said that Cornbread drank one-too-many bottles of carpenter's glue as a kid, and it messed up his head. But, my uncle isn't exactly a medical expert.

And, I might add…I've drank all kinds of glue: hot glue, glass glue, rubber glue…and I'm perfectly fine! So, forgive me if I'm a *tad* skeptical about Cornbread's "glue brains" diagnosis…

He probably took a sheep kick to the mush as a toddler. Which will mess a kid up!

Maybe Cornbread had jumbled brains because he was black? But, I'm not totally sure on that theory either. My buddies Gus and Larry are black, and they're sharp as a tack. So, who knows why Cornbread can't talk right.

For whatever the reason, Cornbread had a limited vocabulary. He could only say one word, "cornbread." Whether it was glue guzzling, or a sheep hoof to the noggin', or just a case of the porridge brains, Cornbread could only say cornbread.

Don't get me wrong, Cornbread was perfectly fine. He was happy, healthy and socially active. Folks loved being around Cornbread. He's probably the best conversationalist I've ever met. The man could capture an audience's attention like Jello in a nursing home. For the most part, he spoke just fine, except he said *cornbread* for every word. And like I said, Cornbread told the best stories!

"Cornbread cornbread," he'd say while smiling with his thick white teeth.

Cornbread's family had that horse money, if you know what I mean. But he never let his wealth go to his head. He was a very generous man. He even let Uncle Shty rent his detached garage for free. As long as Uncle Shty fed Cornbread's dogs every morning: Jet, Queenie, and Duck. Cornbread called them *cornbread* of course, but their collars displayed their names.

Jet and Queenie were both English bullmastiffs. Cornbread kept the sibling dogs outside to watch over the piles of scrap lying around his property.

Duck Dog, as the boys and I called him, was the elder of the three bullmastiffs. When Cornbread was a child, Duck Dog was his saddle-dog. Because of that, Duck Dog got to live in the house.

Jet and Queenie were well over a hundred pounds with solid builds and short dark muzzles that faded into a reddish tan coat. They were big for English bullmastiffs. Duck Dog, however, was a real-life giant. He was a *gen-u-wine* grade A Big Rug bullmastiff. Grade A Big Rug bullmastiffs are rare to come by, and they ain't cheap. Heck…my saddle-dog, Gamb-Balls, was a grade C, and Pops complained for years about how expensive he was.

The bullmastiff was a popular working man's dog back when Truce Deradodo founded Big Rug. He made it town law that:

> *"Thou settlers wishing to take thy homestead in the town of Big Rug, shall only be permitted to bring thy canine, if which thy canine exceeds the weight of one common hen-horse."*

And as most folks know, a common hen-horse—or female grass-sheep if you're west of Mumper—weighs no less than one-hundred-and-twenty pounds. Anything below that weight is considered a regular, run-of-the-mill, house horse.

Over the years of breeding these large dogs, the town of Big Rug unintentionally created a Darwinian incubator for the evolution of the largest dog breed on Earth, the Big Rug bullmastiff! Also known as a saddle-dog.

The first time I went to the city, I learned most folks follow a two-step transportation process. Step one, ride a bicycle as a child; step two, drive a car as an adult. That means city folks don't ever ride-the-saddle. Most of 'em don't even have real dogs. Shook me up pretty good when I saw a lady pull a fluffy dog-rat out of her purse at a bagel shop. Initially, I thought it was an oversized pocket mouse; or some kinda exotic lint-gerbil or something like that... But I asked her, and she confirmed it was a dog.

In Big Rug, we have a four-step transportation process. A saddle-dog from age of three-ish to eight-ish, bicycle from eight-ish to thirteen-ish, the All-Terrain Eight from thirteen-ish to twenty-ish, and finally an automobile. But most folks just keep ridin' an ATV, even after they complete the All-Terrain Eight.

Town law states:

> *"Big Rugians of Big Rug Township must obtain an ATV license (BR-ATV-LIC) and fulfill eight-years of operation with an American National Standards Institute certified ATV before applying for an automobile driver's license."*

The BR-ATV-LIC includes your basic quad, quad-bike, three-wheeler, four-wheeler, quadricycle, quatro-mas-uno, mud-spud, modified mud-spud, click 'n stick gravel cruiser, dirt duster, crotch-rocket with a spurly socket, or a non-modified stacked six-wheeler.

But Big Rug law finds no quarrel in a gentlemen's gas-powered lap-tapper, modified swamper, recreational dune-dasher, ten-speed brush hush without a throttle-bottle, or a pull-and-pop big wheel double-stroke two-cylinder rubber-bubber, if it has a standard steel chassis with welded seams.

Upon completing the All-Terrain Eight, a Big Rugian is free to drive a car. But heck…where's the fun in that? Give me a mod-quad with flappers on the sloppers and a leather tush-cush over a gas pedal four-seater any day of the week!

One day, the boys and I were walking home from elementary school when we found Jet and Queenie rummaging through garbage in the alleyway behind Cornbread's house. To say it startled us would be an understatement.

We'd never seen them unchained without Cornbread to keep them in line. I knew we were in trouble the second they looked up at us and lost interest in the chicken bones they'd found in the trash. Junkyard dogs don't easily part with chicken bones.

It was Beef Jerky While You Worky Day at school, so we were loaded up with fresh flavors of jerky to munch on. Jet and Queenie could smell us coming from a mile away. Nothing gets a couple of junkyard dogs riled up like the scent of flavored meats.

Saliva dripped from their mouths as they licked their chops and slowly walked closer. Each step of the massive beasts sent waves of terror through the alleyway. We stood there, frozen in place, fearing that the slightest movement might be our last.

Gus, however, must not have been as terrified as the rest of us. He slowly lowered his head—puckered out his lips like a fat woodpecker—and corralled a jerky stick that was poking out of his shirt pocket. He tugged it into his mouth with a perk-and-pull motion of the lips while the rest of his body remained motionless.

Even Jet and Queenie watched in amazement. Once Gus maneuvered the entire jerky stick into his mouth, he rotated his eyes over to us boys and whispered, "Beef cigar."

Gus's voice triggered Jet and Queenie to attack. Gravel flew back from the force of their heavy paws as they struggled to gain traction on the dirt path. My life flashed before my eyes as I watched the enormous beasts barreling toward us boys.

And then, out of nowhere, Duck Dog came bursting through the wooden fence separating Cornbread's yard from the alleyway. He looked like a superhero exploding through a building.

Wood panels and splinters went flying through the air as he tackled the charging dogs to the ground. After a few seconds of intense skirmishing, Jet and Queenie retreated back to their kennels with their tails between their legs.

The boys and I slapped each other high-fives while hugging Duck Dog; thanking him for saving our lives. He was like a hero from that moment on. Duck Dog, the king of the alleyway! And king of the number-two-pee-yews if you know what I mean? The smell of a fresh duck-log could knock the wind out of an elephant.

When I was a toddler, I stepped in a duck-log that squished all the way up my calf. I was bouncin' round on my fat baby feet in the springtime grass—stumbling after honey-flies as they buzzed down a dandelion path—and *wham-o;* duck-log…up to my calf! The stench lingered on my skin for weeks. Mama denies it, but my Aunt Sara told me that Pops asked the doctor to amputate my leg because it smelled so bad. Probably not my father's finest parenting moment.

The day after our near-death experience, the boys and I told every listening ear how Duck Dog, the king of the alleyway, saved our lives from the villainous Jet and Queenie.

Rumors had been circulating around town that the Huggabee sisters were eaten alive by Jet and Queenie three weeks earlier. So, to honor the memory of those poor girls, I reminded my classmates of the Huggabees' gruesome fate.

"Three weeks before Jet and Queenie tried to eat us boys," I dramatically told a group of kids during school lunch, "the two dogs went on a hunger-fueled rampage, eating everything in sight.

"They ate chickens; they ate coon-cats; they ate garbage meat; but no matter how much they consumed; nothing satisfied their carnal cravings. And that's when they spotted the Huggabees walking home from Bible study. Jet and Queenie swallowed them up with a single bite."

I chomped into my ham sandwich and whispered ominously, "All that was left was Andrea Huggabee's back brace."

"It's true," Suzie LaCuzzi spoke softly. "I have English class with Andrea and Haley. Miss Grittle takes role every morning before class. One day, she just stopped calling for the Huggabees."

Marie-Agnus stepped forward confidently and added, "The Huggabees were definitely eaten by Cornbread's dogs. Those girls always had bubble gum on their shoes. Dogs love bubble gum... The Huggabees didn't stand a chance."

The group of kids standing around my lunch table began gossiping. I knew my story was hitting a nerve when Big Rig Bevy— a gal with tree trunks for legs—pushed her lunch away in disgust.

"Most of us thought the Huggabees fell in the sinkhole behind the Big Rug Magazine Library and Coupon Trading Post," Suzie admitted. "But it makes a lot more sense that they were eaten by Jet and Queenie. Especially if they had bubble gum on their shoes."

Big Rig Bevy and a few other girls comforted each other as the group grew silent, saddened by the loss of our dear friends.

"Our mother remarried!" Haley Huggabee shrieked through the crowd, causing all of us to jump in fright.

That girl literally scared the crap out of me that day... And I've never told a soul until right now.... I just stood up—without sayin' a word to no one—walked straight to the restroom, threw my soiled undies in the trash, and acted like nothin' ever happened on the day Haley Huggabee scared the crap out of me. Well...technically, I guess her name was Haley Zapinsky after her mother got remarried.

But I swear—and all the boys will attest to this—that summer, something happened to the Huggabees. They may not have been eaten alive by Jet and Queenie, but when school let out that summer, those girls were stick figures, and when school started in the fall, they had curves like a roll'e coast'e… And their last name changed… So sue me if I just assumed, like everyone else in town, they were dead!

Ronny's father, Mayor Bill "Billy-Boy" Deradodo, was so thankful Duck Dog saved our lives that he used his mayor power to rename the alleyway behind Cornbread's house, *Duck Dog Alleyway*.

During the alleyway ceremony, Coach uninvitingly stumbled his way onto stage and presented Duck Dog with a key to the stadium to wear on his collar, which was more symbolic than functional. Big Rug Stadium is just a couple dozen folding chairs in the field behind Cheese on Cheese, Yes & Please, Brunch Bistro and Manners School. The key was actually Coach's key to his mom's trailer—which he subsequently found himself locked out of that evening.

My aunt Sara wanted to do something special too. To show her appreciation, she made an "official" Duck Dog sweater that people could rent for fancy events. It was "official" because she sewed it out of his hair. It was a beautiful sweater; and gender neutral!

Mayor Deradodo also ordered that all the Big Rug public buildings must set out a bowl of dog food every morning, so that Duck Dog could eat while roaming around town. All the dog food sitting outside caused some serious issues with critters, but like my grampy used to say, "Sometimes the price, is a head full of lice."

Jet, Queenie, and Duck Dog all passed away while the boys and I were in high school. Duck Dog was the first to go. He died from obesity. The dog food sitting around town wasn't Mayor Deradodo's best idea.

It seemed like everyone had a story to tell at Duck Dog's funeral. But it was Cornbread's eulogy that brought a tear to my eye. With grace in a time of sorrow, that hillbilly redneck looked up from the podium and eloquently said, "Cornbread! Cornbread cornbread."

Chokes me up just thinkin' 'bout it.

I have an older sister named Boof who chipped her front tooth. She was helping my grampy frame a shed when she took a two-by-four to the mush. We never found her front chomper. I found a pebble that looked a lot like her tooth though… Mama helped Boof super glue it to her tooth nub. But after a while, it just looked like Boof had a rock tooth. "There goes Boof with her rock toof," folks would say.

Even Mr. McGilbert down at The Manhole Diner—named after his once successful, but now unlawful, refurbished manhole cover business—tried to help Boof fix her tooth. He sat a half-gallon mason jar next to the cash register with a sign that read, *"Boof's Toof Jar,"* in hopes of raising enough money to have a concrete artisan—or talented wood whittler—make a tooth for Boof. But folks mostly filled Boof's Toof Jar with buttons and baby teeth.

After a few weeks, Mr. McGilbert had to bury the jar. A jar full of baby teeth creates an incredibly foul odor; like burnt hair sautéed in spoiled milk. Not even the greasy aroma of The Manhole could hide the stench.

For years, Boof would go out to the shed and look for her tooth. Gently sliding her finger tips across the ground, carefully moving the stones and pebbles from side to side. There was nothing that Boof desired more than the missing piece of her tooth.

In the rain and the sun, Boof looked for her tooth. While us boys played and had fun, Boof looked for her tooth. On Christmas Day and the Fourth of July, Boof looked for her tooth with a tear in her eye. When her chores were complete, and her homework was done, Boof looked for her tooth, like a game never won.

The missing tooth, lost on the ground, caused Boof misery, as it lay unfound. What she desired, is what made her sad. Even in good times, Boof still felt bad.

Boof could finish first, she could get a grade A; but even in victory, Boof still felt the same. Until one day, I heard Boof say, "To find my tooth…there is no way."

And just like that, on a cool fall day, Boof stopped her search, and walked away. It ended as fast as it started. Like a car window rolling down after Grampa has farted.

Twenty years later, Boof and I opened a working man's glove store in town called Jesus Hands, *"Leather gloves so strong, not even a nail can go through them."* Boof sews 'em, I sell 'em! We make a good team. Jesus Hands leather gloves are in the back pocket of almost every city worker in town. We even offer a replacement warranty if your gloves get too "holy."

I always wondered if Jesus wore a ponytail when he was carpentering? If he did…then he was one cool dude. No doubt!

You sure don't hear a lot about Jesus's time workin' construction. I mean, don't get me wrong, I really appreciate all the paintings of Jesus healing people, or sitting around and looking at the clouds; but how about a painting of Jesus shimmied up on a lumber frame tying in a strut to a king post? I'm sure the man took pride in his work. Seems like we oughta celebrate his craftsmanship a little more.

Boof and I don't talk much about the missing piece of her tooth these days, or why she abruptly stopped looking for it. I've always thought it was odd though. For so long she was obsessed with finding it. And then, one day, she wasn't.

Mama told me, "A man can go crazy trying to understand the mind of a woman, but he'd be crazy not to try."

And Pops used to say, "Trying to understand a woman is like trying to figure out what color the letter five smells like."

I guess what I'm saying is, folks are complicated.

So, who knows why Boof stopped looking for her tooth? Who knows why Jet and Queenie ate those poor Huggabee girls? Who knows why city folks don't ride-the-saddle as toddlers? Or why artists don't paint murals of Jesus in a tool belt carpentering the crap outta some timber? Who knows why people do anything really?

It's just like my dear old grampy used to say, "You don't know 'til you eat the broth of another man's stew. You just need the appetite to understand."

Roots on the river have no fear of a drought.

— Ormish scripture

A BRIEF HISTORY

In the fall of 1832, a young, ambitious, amateur aviator flew his red and gold hot air balloon from the northwest corridor's southern tip to the central territory's eastern parcel. On that trip, Ronny's super-great grandfather—Truce Deradodo—discovered an undeveloped valley of the forest. When Truce returned home, he said that looking down on the valley from his hot air balloon was like looking down on a "big rug" of brightly colored trees.

Truce was a tall, slender, clumsy kid who came from a family of stocking cap makers. The kind of hats with the little ball on top. Most folks figured he'd grow up and take over the family business. Others thought he'd go to work as an apple orchard picker, a common line of work for tall young men in his village at the time. Even more folks figured he'd die young—like most of the Deradodo men—from an injury incurred by clumsiness.

They call it the Deradodo Clumsy Curse. Back when Truce was a boy, the average life expectancy of a Deradodo male was twenty-four. The most common cause of death was tripping. A tall man tripping on a cobblestone street is an ungraceful sight.

All the Deradodo men are clumsy. Ronny's father refuses to go fishing because he can't bait a hook without sticking his thumb. The man once had a fishhook stuck in his thumb for two months.

"Leave it be," he shouted when Dr. Gozer offered to remove the hook. "It'll work its way out! Already lost a pinky toe to a fish hook. Not gonna lose a thumb too!"

To everyone's surprise, Truce forwent his claim to the Deradodo family business and returned to the central territory's eastern parcel and founded the town of Big Rug; the first development in the Dustfog Region. Over a century later, the Deradodo legacy is still alive and well in the town of Big Rug. A Deradodo has been mayor every year since its founding, and the family owns some of the most prominent businesses in town.

Truce's wife opened the very first business in town: The Lady Eyebrow Emporium. And they're still splitting unibrows into double brows today!

Back when my parents were kids, Hank Deradodo, Ronny's uncle, began converting old septic tanks into storm shelters. Today, Septic Safe is a powerhouse in the storm-shelter market.

Hank is probably the most influential Deradodo, other than Truce. Folks around town say that Truce may have founded the town of Big Rug, but Hank put us on the map.

Hank's a fancy man who knows math and stuff. He organized some outside investors to fund the prestigious Clowns Don't Frown Culinary Arts Institute; the only school in the region that offers a dual certification in both clown studies and the culinary arts. My cousin Fannie graduated with almost a B average! He wears his CDFCAI hat every day...

Across the front it reads, *"These Clowns Can Cook!"*

On the last day of ninth grade, Big Gut Gus snuck up behind me and kicked my books out of my hands right in front of a group of smokin' hot betties.

"Book-check!" Gus yelled, while kids laughed at my loose papers floating down around me like oversized pieces of confetti.

As I gathered my scattered schoolwork on the floor, Ronny walked by and slipped on my yearbook.

"Captain Klutz at it again," I heard Gus cackle while running down the hall.

As Ronny rolled on the ground, moaning in pain, he grabbed my yearbook, opened it to the front page and scribbled, *"If you eat gum, you chew gum!"*

It was a somewhat legendary phrase to us boys. When we were younger, it was just fun to say before swallowing gum after a good chew. But as time passed, we realized there was a little wisdom in that silly saying.

Ronny learned the phrase from his mother's side of the family. Every Thanksgiving, Ronny's grandpappy and granduncle would argue about who clogged the toilet after Thanksgiving dinner.

"Your brother isn't welcome in this home," Grandpappy demanded to Ronny's grandmother. "The man collects plungers, don't ya know?

"Jimpsten," Grandpappy shouted and shook his fat old man finger of judgment at Ronny's granduncle. "I know it's the holidays…but you're a toilet clogger damn it! And this whole family knows it. If you eat gum, you chew gum! And I'm not paying for a plumber. I gots my limits!"

The day the boys and I graduated high school, I cut out the front page of my ninth-grade year book, framed it, and gave it to Ronny as a graduation gift.

"If you eat gum, you chew gum!" Framed in glass so the memory will last!

Ronny certainly got his quirkiness from his mother's side of the family, but his pride came from his father's side. The boy was a Deradodo through 'n' through! And he never missed an opportunity to remind us boys that Truce Deradodo was his *super*-great grandfather. Every day—hot or cold—Ronny wore a stocking cap with one of those little fluffy balls on top, because that's what his *super*-great grandfather wore.

"Some heroes wear capes. Some heroes wear caps," he'd boast while sweat soaked through his thick cotton hat in the summer sun. "And...if used by Truce, it must have a use! People say that you know... It's a thing."

Turns out those little fluffy balls on top of stocking caps do have a use. Back in the day, sailors wore hats with a fluffy ball on top to alert them of something overhead. Kinda like cat whiskers. It helped them gauge the height of the boat's cabin and protected their heads from unexpected bumps.

Maybe that's why the Deradodo's were in the stocking cap business back in the 1800's? It could've been less about the money, and more about surviving the Deradodo Clumsy Curse. When you're an accident-prone family, you'd better have head protection. And Lord knows Ronny, a.k.a. Captain Klutz, was a Deradodo doof just like the rest of the men in his family.

"Blood red is Ronny's favorite color," Dale always teased with a laugh. "The Deradodo Clumsy Curse keeps trying, but Captain Klutz keeps surviving."

"At least I wear shoes with laces," Ronny countered, pointing at Dale's house slippers.

"The rubber bands *act* as laces, you dork-cork."

Dale fell and hit his head as a kid when his shoelaces got caught on a tree root. He almost died. After that day, he refused to wear laces. He only wore house slippers with rubber bands around them.

The near-death experience kinda worked out in Dale's favor though. First, he got an awesome scar on the back of his head. Second, folks love asking him about how he survived the near-death experience. He's probably the closest thing to a local celebrity we have around town. And third, the betties love a man with a good story, and Dale has a story that the betties love to hear.

"The only reason you got into log rolling," Dale continued bickering with Ronny, "is because no one would dare put an axe in your hands. Lumberjacking and the Deradodo Clumsy Curse don't exactly go well together."

When Ronny was a kid, Dr. Gozer and Dr. Plakas agreed, "Ain't no one ever died from water." So, it was their medical opinion—because of Ronny's clumsiness—that he should enroll in log rolling instead of a traditional axe wielding lumberjack activity for his high school PE requirements. It was the "safe choice."

I guess the wise doctors overlooked the fact that people drown in water…often. There was no such thing as a safe choice when it came to Captain Klutz. Ronny always found a way to smack, bounce, or slap the log while falling into the water.

If there's one thing Ronny taught us boys, other than how long a person can be left unconscious under water without drowning, it's that victory isn't always found in accomplishments. Often, victory is found in the courage to try, even with the certainty of defeat. Ronny doesn't always succeed…but he's always triumphant! Because he has the courage to try.

Ronny started collecting fossils in the fourth grade. He wanted to be a "gynecologist," as he put it. He later learned that the proper pronunciation of his new found interest was "geologist," but not before giving a *"What I want to be when I grow up,"* presentation to our fourth-grade class.

Mrs. Boil wasn't amused when Ronny stood up and said, "I want to be a *gynecologist* when I grow up. Because I like getting my hands dirty." The boys and I teased him for months after that presentation. Ronny, the gynecological geologist! Exploring new holes every day!

Three years later, Ronny found a rock in the town of Low Water that he swore was a fossil. Low Water sits in the wet lands between the northern border of Stoolmist and the southern base of Mrs. Yoder's Mountain.

It's a small Ormish town comprised of rice paddy fields with little stone bridges connecting one field to the other. The Ormish, or, "Oriental Amish" if you're a Highgrass fancy Dutch traditionalist, own the rice market like Mumper owns the pumpkin market! Or how Big Rug owns the critter market. I suppose everyone in the Dustfog Region offers something... Stoolmist owns the market on being birdy-turdy sneaker-squeakers who lumberjack like fellas with shaved armpits! That's not an opinion, that's a fact! You can ask anyone.

Ronny would shove the rock in our faces and say, "Smell it! It smells like rotten eggs. That's how you know it's a fossil."

"Does that mean Gus's feet are fossils?" Dale joked.

"Athlete's foot isn't a joke," Gus snapped. "You wouldn't know *Dale,* you're not an athlete! Only athletes have athlete's foot," he demanded, rolling the jerky stick in his mouth from left to right and tugging down on his leather workin' man's gloves.

Gus always wore his dad's leather work gloves when we were kids. They were like shoes for his hands.

"Gonna be a workin' man," he'd say while pushing up his chubby cheeks with a smile.

"You have athlete's foot because you don't wash your socks," Dale reminded Gus.

"They… Don't… Need… Washed! I've told you a million times, they're extra absorbent."

Ronny interrupted the athlete's foot argument and held his Low Water rock up in the air.

"When invertebrates died a billion years ago, they fossilized in the mud. A billion years ago there was a lot of sulfur in the ground… That's why some fossils smell like rotten eggs," he exclaimed while we mostly ignored him.

"Smells more like a turd to me," Mitch interjected while combing back his thick black hair.

Chad agreed, "The rock *does* look like a turd Ronny."

"Yawp," Brant blurted while building a campfire.

"It's not a turd," Ronny barked. "Just focus on the fire Brant!"

Brant knew more about fire than a skintag knows a fat-fold.

"It's all about the fire triangle," he'd explain while tying back his knotted hair locks. "Oxygen, heat, and fuel to warm up what's cool."

Brant was Ormish on his mother's side of the family. His father traveled from Plumpstin City to Green Wind Stream on a fishing trip. While at the stream he met an Ormish woman. The two fell in love, got married, moved to Big Rug, and the rest is history.

He had the olive skin, narrow eyes, and thick silky black hair of the Ormish, which he wore in the form of thirty-two knotted hair locks that he'd pull up into a bun. His locks of hair represented the original Ormish hex sign, or "barn star" if you're a Highgrass fancy Dutch traditionalist. The hex sign is an image of thirty-two interlocked frogs to form the shape of a dragon.

The frogs represent the original thirty-two settlers who came down from Mrs. Yoder's Mountain and survived The Decade of the Dragon before the village of Low Water was developed.

I always thought it'd be cool if Brant had red hair like his father. Back when my grandparents were young, there was an old wives' tale about the good fortune of seeing a redheaded Ormish person. It was believed that upon seeing a redheaded Ormish person, an individual would be immune to sunburn for a year. Melanoma put an end to that superstition.

My granny used to tell Boof and I all kinds of old wives' tales when we were kids. Things like, *"Soaking your toes in varnish helps with allergies,"* or *"Cottage cheese breast milk is an aphrodisiac."* I actually heard Granny tell Mama that one.

Initially, I mistakenly thought Granny was saying "Afro Jesiac." I thought they were talkin' 'bout black Jesus… Or Jesus's black cousin or something? Either way, I wanted to meet the dude! So, I swiped some breastmilk from Dale's house when his mom was farmin' boobs with his baby brother. Breastmilk doesn't cottage cheese like you'd think. And the texture is definitely a deal breaker!

Granny's favorite old wives' tale was, *"Dancing everyday keeps your hair from turning gray."* So, Granny was always groovin'.

Heck… Granny was the one who took Boof and I to our first concert. We saw Bozo Goober and the Spoons in the Spotlight perform in the gravel lot behind Sugar Lips. Bozo Goober…man, that guy can slap the spoons!

When we walked up to the show, we saw two stubble-rubbers dancin' to Bozo's majestical musical compositions. The way those two fellas floated across the dance floor was remarkable. I swear, at one point I saw them levitate off the ground. I always knew gaywads were special, but I recon they might be magical too…

Watching those two limp wrists dance was like being at a fancy Broadway show. Granny was so moved by their fancy dancin' that she invited them to join us inside Sugar Lips. And, we got *three* scoops of gelato for the price of *one!* One scoop turning into three… If that's not magic, I don't know what is!

After high school, Ronny got a degree in Public Works and returned to town to work as a councilman. On the weekends, he taught Saturday school for the seniors needing extra help to graduate. It's also where he met his wife, Barb Bianchi.

Barb's parents immigrated from Belluno, a small town in Italy about sixty miles north of Venice. Her father, Piero, managed a coal mine down south in Chigger Bottom. After incurring a serious leg injury in the mines, Piero washed his hands of the coal business and opened a gelato parlor in Big Rug called Sugar Lips.

The only thing more impressive than Piero's gelato is his mustache. The man has more hair on his top lip than most men have on their entire body. His mustache is so dense, it's water proof.
I once watched the man taste test syrup, and his mustache left scratch marks on the wooden spoon.

You'd think a mustache that dangerous would be a mood killer between the sheets! But, Mr. and Mrs. Bianchi found a way; because the summer us boys went into the sixth grade the Bianchi's had a baby girl named Barb.

Us boys never dreamed that one day Ronny would fall in love with little Barb Bianchi while teaching her in Saturday school. I suppose you could say that they were high school sweethearts. The two were in high school when they met... For different reasons of course. But still...

A teacher-student romance qualifies as a high school love story in my opinion. Love is complicated... And Barb was really mature for her age.

There's a saying, *"You don't know someone 'til you've walked a mile in their shoes."* Well, in Big Rug, when a young man proposes to a young lady, it's tradition that he wear a pair of her shoes and walk a mile in them. Just like the saying says to do.

A fella will typically walk from his house to the lucky lady's house—in a pair of her shoes—and then proposes. We call it the "Love Walk." My wife Brekanny gets teary-eyed every time she sees a young man grinning ear to ear while taking the Love Walk. Heck, I'll even admit, seeing a dude stumblin' round in high heels touches a soft spot in my heart too. What can I say? I'm a romantic, I guess.

On the day of Barb's graduation, Ronny walked up on stage wearing a pair of her spray-painted purple high heels, dropped to one knee and said, "Ouch... Dang it! I should've worn my knee-pads."

The Deradodo Clumsy Curse knows no bounds...

"Sweet-cheeks," Ronny winced in pain. "I've walked a mile in your shoes; and I twisted my ankle twice while doing so. I don't want to walk another mile without you by my side. Barbara Bianchi, will you make me the happiest man in this whole dang high school graduation and marry me?"

Barb said yes, put the ring on her finger, turned to Principal Keck, and accepted her high school diploma *slash* 30% off coupon to Don't Drink Paint Supply.

Today, we've come to learn that Big Rug's Love Walk tradition is a major contributor to the plantar wart epidemic in town. It's how I got my warts. Brekanny has hot feet! Lots of sweating... But, when you marry someone, you marry them, warts and all.

Ronny was promoted to city council president shortly after he married Barb. His staple accomplishment was securing funding to fix the Ferris Wheel Chapel that'd been out of service for almost a year. We were having to attend church out at Lake Sippo in the fish-cleaning canopy. Sometimes, going to church just stinks! Especially when it's in a fish-cleaning canopy.

But Ronny saved the day. Now, every Sunday, Big Rugians can listen to the word of God while enjoying a ride on the Ferris Wheel Chapel. It really adds to the emotion of the service. You want a spiritual awakening? Go get your worship on while weightlessly rotating to the sound of carnival music.

Ronny also revived the Walk on Water Wednesday Worship; which is every Wednesday evening, in the month of July, at the Big Rug Public Pool and Baptism Pond.

The service was stopped back when us boys were in high school because of a wheelchair accessibility issue. The issue was that the ushers accidently rolled some old folks into the pool.

I thought them geriatrics were flailing around in the water because they were "touched" by the Holy Spirit or something… Turns out they were just drowning. I swear it sounded like they were talking in tongues though.

Thank God oxygen tanks are buoyant! Those blue hairs popped outta the water like Russian submarines. *"Save the oldies,"* people screamed in a panic while jumping in the water. Preacher Jepp says that, "technically," he baptized everyone who got wet that day. The Lord works in mysterious ways, I guess.

Folks were pretty upset for a while. But Ronny secured funding for bumper rails around the pool, eliminating the wheelchair accessibility issue. And just like that, Walk on Water Wednesday Worship was back in session. Church in a pool really makes a man appreciate the Lord's divine creations. Brekanny's worship bikini is a heavenly sight if I've ever seen one!

My Uncle Shty had a buddy named Muhck, who was in the critter business when the boys and I were kids. Muhck's Critter Sitter, *"I'll hold 'em, 'til you've sold 'em."* Nice little critter storage business if you ask me.

Critter auctions are every Sunday after church in the field next to the Big Rug Public Pool and Baptism Pond. But if the Ferris Wheel Chapel isn't spinnin', the critter business isn't winnin'. Simply put, if folks aren't on the worship wheel, they aren't attending the critter auction after church.

Kids love critters, betties love critters, even stubborn old Redman used to smile when he'd see a moosemunk sunbathing on his rocking chair. Squirrels, skunks, coon-cats, gofers, mud-moles, corn-rats, fur-necked frogs; if it's a critter, you'll find it at the critter auction.

A loving father will buy a little house-critter for the kids after church, the critter escapes into the attic, the father pays for the critter to be trapped—transferring the critter's ownership rights to the critter catcher—the critter catcher then sells the critter to the critter auction, who then sells the critter to the public. Most likely to a loving father trying to replace the critter that got away. It's a cyclical business for sure!

Muhck knew everything about the critter business. At fourteen years of age, he started Muhck's Critter Sitter with his friend Mimi; a gal who looks like an ostrich with the face of a retarded bulldog. She and Muhck look good together though…

One time, us boys were at my Uncle Shty's shop while Muhck explained some of the intricacies of the critter business.

"See na see, you gots three branches of the critter bidness." Muhck babbled, holding up two fingers on one hand, and a half thumb on the other.

"First, you gots the critter catcher. Dangerous game the critter catcher play. Lost my thumb catchin' critters.

"Once a critter caught, the critter catcher stores the critter. Storin' critters the second part. Because critter catchers don't store critters… That be ridiculous. They two different bidness models. Like overalls and pantyhose. Both clothes, but very different.

"Catch a critter Tuesday, gotta store it 'til Sunday… Because Sunday, the Critter Auction. Critter Auction the last part, see na see."

Muhck smiled with his missing front teeth and let out a gargling belch under his breath.

"Critter this, critter that. Critter bats, critter rats. Critter dusk, critter dawn. Critter caught, critter gone.

"Customer pay to *catch* the critter, critter catcher pay to *store* the critter, auction pay to *sell* the critter, customer pay to *buy* the critter. For moneys, you see… First rule of bidness; gotta spend moneys to make moneys.

"That mean the critter *catcher* makin' the moneys. Critter *storer* makin' the moneys. Critter auction makin' the moneys. Everyone makin' the moneys. One, two, three, see na see… It's bidness!"

Muhck was smart when it came to critters, but he wasn't very successful as a business owner. Mimi was a poor manager, and Muhck was a poor worker. So financially…they were poor. But they did enough to make ends meet.

Now, if you want to talk about profitability, Crawl Space Critters had that horse money! They were rollin' in the dough like a saddle-dog in the snow. But, like my grampy used to mumble when he'd lose his dentures, "Mo money, mo problems…"

The "problems" surrounding Crawl Space Critters stemmed from the controversial owners, the Druker triplets of Mumper. If you're a Mumponian, your business is pumpkins, not critters. But the Druker triplets took another path, and it paid off, big time!

Durff, Grumb, and Prich-May were round gals. There wasn't a pointy part on their entire bodies. You've heard of curves in "all the right places?" Well, the Druker girls had curves in "all the places." Good lookin' gals though! I always thought Grumb was easy on the eyes. And man could they critter! Folks used to say their red hair and freckles hypnotized critters, putting them in a daze and making them easier to catch.

Crawl Space Critters may have been the largest critter-catching service in the region, but Big Rugians stick with their own. Which is why Skunk Weasel's Junior Varsity Football Critter Catch has always done well in town. To play junior varsity football, students have to volunteer one week a month for the critter catching service. The proceeds fund the school's football program.

Although Skunk Weasel's Junior Varsity Football Critter Catch is limited to just Big Rug, they get plenty of business. Big Rug is a critter hot spot due to the towns deep trash layers in the soil.

Critter Quitters is another local Big Rug operation. The Horschadech boys inherited the business from their father, Bobby, when he died from a heart attack while shimmying down Miss Poterspeel's chimney after a coon-cat. To this day, Bobby Horschadech is the only Big Rugian to ever be cremated.

When someone dies in Big Rug, we follow a traditional, "Day of Display," where the body is placed in the front yard of the deceased, so folks can drive by and take a gander. Then comes the "Pray for a Day" at church, immediately followed by a "Buried in Hay" ceremony at the Big Rug Cemetery and Pee-Wee Football Field.

I was just a kid when it happened, but I remember the town going to great lengths trying to get Bobby's body out of that chimney.

Sheriff Beitzel tried to lasso Bobby and pull him out. But Bobby's Adam's apple beard got snagged on the flue side of the damper.

"Bobby ain't budgin," the sheriff yelled from the rooftop.

Mayor Deradodo paid a magician to try and levitate Bobby's body outta that dang chimney. But the magician said there was something about the "type of shingles" on the house that canceled out his magical powers.

After several days of failed efforts, folks were running low on ideas on how to retrieve Bobby's body from Miss Poterspeel's chimney. The final attempt was when The Manhole donated a barrel of breakfast grease to pour down the chimney.

"Grease up Bobby's body," Mayor Deradodo shouted. "At night, the world spins upside down. Bobby's body will slide right on outta that chimney," he educated the folks standing around the house.

"Billy-Boy," our science teacher politely interjected. "That's not quite how it works. Gravity pulls us to the ground even when the Earth is upside down."

"If you's 'a rhymin', you's 'a lyin'." Sheriff Beitzel said, putting one finger to his nose while pointing at Mr. Stoltzer with the other.

"I'm not lying," Mr. Stoltzer pleaded. "We don't fall out of bed at night because the world spins upside down."

"No way to know," the mayor responded, gently sliding his hand on Mr. Stoltzer's shoulder. "We's asleep."

Three days of greasing, and Bobby's body didn't move an inch. He actually slid further down into the chimney from what I heard… Sheriff Beitzel was right, Bobby wasn't budgin'.

So, like my grampy used to say, "When all else fails and it's time to retire, strike a match and light a fire."

And that's how Bobby Horschadech became the first, and only, Big Rugian to be cremated.

Whether it was fixing the Ferris Wheel Chapel, bringing back Walk on Water Wednesday Worship, or supporting the critter business, it's safe to say Ronny did a great job as an elected official. So great, that when his father retired as Mayor of Big Rug, Ronny had more than enough support from the town to be our next leader.

Ronny's the best Mayor Big Rug has ever had in my humble opinion. And he gave one of the most beautiful acceptance speeches at his inauguration. I still have his note cards. He threw them on the ground in frustration after enduring several paper cuts during the speech. The Deradodo Clumsy Curse keeps trying, but Ronny keeps surviving.

"In Big Rug we have a saying," Ronny began the speech. "What climbs up, must climb down."

It was the perfect opener, and exemplified Ronny's deep connection with the town. *"What climbs up, must climb down,"* is like gospel to Big Rugians.

Round these parts, it's common for a child to climb a tree, become frightened, and end up having to stay in the tree until they muster up the courage to climb down. Typically, a kid will climb down within an hour or so. But sometimes, it can take weeks for a child to overcome their fears.

We call them "tree kids." Messy little devils if you park your car under one. A bird crapping on your car is one thing, but a tree kid; windshield wiper fluid just ain't gonna cut it!

No matter how many days and nights are spent in a tree, a child must climb down by their own accord. Only the child can find the courage to conquer their fear. A concerned neighbor or fireman with a ladder can't do that for them. *"What climbs up, must climb down."*

And just like it takes courage for a tree kid to climb down from their branchy trappings, it takes courage to be the Mayor of Big Rug. And what man has more courage than a Deradodo man?

Ronny ended his speech by saying, "I'll work every day for this town, or I'll die trying. I am both; a Big Rugian...and a Deradodo!"

For Ronny, that's his reality and his secret weapon. Whatever Captain Klutz is doing, the Deradodo Clumsy Curse might kill him while doing it.

I once watched Ronny dislocate his shoulder while swatting at a fly. A few years back Ronny fractured his nose while putting on his church suspenders. Heck, he twists his ankle several times a year just getting out of bed in the morning. So, I guess when you're expecting a hard fall, it's a little easier to get back up. And as long as I've known him, Ronny has always gotten back up.

To this day, I feel a sense of pride when walking up the brick stairway of the Big Rug Town Hall and Drive-Thru Deli and see "Mayor Ronny Deradodo" on the glass door at the end of the hallway. If you were to open that door, you'd see a dark wooden desk with a stocking cap resting on top of a lamp. And behind the desk, hanging on the wall, framed in glass so the memory will last, you'd see the first page of my ninth-grade year book,

"If you eat gum, you chew gum!"

The guiding motto of a man with good judgement.

Good habits,
   formed from bad experiences,
      are gifts rarely celebrated.

   — Ormish scripture

BULL RABBIT

"I was walking down the second hand produce isle at Thrifty Foods," Dale's mother confided in Mama one night over dinner. "And a woman from out of town walked right up to me and asked, 'Is it true what happened to your son?'

"I couldn't believe it. All I wanted was to shop for gently-used tomatoes in peace. I should've never let the *Big Rug Repository* do that story about Dale. Folks all the way east in Plumpstin City are talking about him."

The day Dale graced the cover of the *Big Rug Repository* was the day that everything changed for him, his family, and us boys. Brant used to say that Dale had the story that the storytellers tell. Brant was right about that one. No doubt!

Even today, all these years later, folks are still fascinated with Dale's story. If you want to hear it first hand, you simply have to enjoy a hearty breakfast at The Manhole. Dale works part-time as a waiter at the diner and is always entertaining guests with his story.

I swear you can smell that greasy spoon from five blocks away. It's like Heaven's air vents are pumping down the scent of sausage on the town of Big Rug. I've personally never preferred the smell of breakfast food. Call me when The Manhole starts cooking canned dog food! Now that's something I could smell all day!

The Manhole is a cornerstone of Big Rug culture. And the owner, Mr. McGilbert, has a long history within the Dustfog Region, dating back to the late nineteenth century when the Central Pacific Railroad was being built out west.

In the early summer of 1867, with the mountains still snowcapped, the Oriental immigrants building the Central Pacific Railway went on strike, resulting in a group of sixty men fleeing their encampment. After weeks of traveling east, they found themselves stranded in the low hills of Mrs. Yoder's Mountain.

The Yoderian Amish, who occupied the mountain, came down from their hidden village of Highgrass—located deep within the Crown of Mrs. Yoder's Mountain—for the first time in over a century. They saved the withered railmen, and brought them back to the village of Highgrass.

Different languages, different cultures, and a shared skepticism of one another, resulted in segregated living. But still, friendships formed, respect was reciprocated, and young love blossomed between the two groups in the misty peaks of the mountain.

However, the intermingling caused tensions between the Highgrass fancy Dutch traditionalists—who preferred separate living conditions—and those who wanted integration. The dispute led to thirty-two individuals descending from the mountain, and into the dismal emptiness of the wetlands of Mrs. Yoder's southern base.

For ten years, the group of thirty-two struggled to survive. The conditions were brutal. Humid and hot in the summer, windy and cold in the winter. The swamp lands couldn't be farmed, and the group of descenders struggled to develop homesteads better than shack-tents.

Three people died in the first year and the rest fell sick to water-mite fever. Those that survived, called themselves "Ormish," a representation of the blended "oriental" and "Amish" cultures.

Then, Gilbert McGilbert—Mr. McGilbert's grandfather—bought the wetlands. He figured since folks were already living on the land, he could make an easy profit by developing a community for them. Gilbert McGilbert called his new community, Low Water.

Today, Low Water is still a predominantly Ormish community, and the McGilberts are still changing lives; down at The Manhole… one breakfast plate at a time.

In the early morning bustle of The Manhole, you'll find Dale with a damp towel in his back pocket—decaf in one hand and regular in the other—telling his story. He still wears his house slippers with rubber bands around them, just like when we were kids. Listeners gaze upon Dale like a kindergardening teacher showing shovels to their students.

Dale's fame came from being one of the few people to come face-to-face with a mythical legend that sits at the top of the folklore food chain in the Dustfog Region: Bull Rabbit. Archeological records show that long before Truce Deradodo discovered the region, the natives of this land had been seeing a giant rabbit in Big Rug's forested valley for decades.

Town elders tell tales that speak of an oversized male bunny who rules the animal kingdom of the Dustfog Region. Brant's father, Earl—the Chief Park Ranger of Owdina National Park—estimates that Bull Rabbit probably weighs around seventy pounds, and if stretched out, could be up to five feet in length.

Every year, there's a farmer or two who blames Bull Rabbit for eating up an acre's worth of crops. My grampy used to say, "Ain't nothin' funny 'bout a bunny eatin' money." An acre's worth of crops can feed a town for months. But everyone knows if your crops are eaten, it's almost always by a herd of moosemunks.

Those dang moosemunks can destroy an acre's worth of crops in one night. And if it's not moosemunks, then it's probably a pack of coon-cats or a flock of badger birds… But not Bull Rabbit. Earl says a rabbit that size would only eat the shadecane growing on creek banks, not farm crops.

A handful of folks claim they've seen a giant rabbit while walking a wooded path. Even more have stepped in—or collected—rabbit droppings the size of golf balls. And from time to time someone comes across a rabbit footprint the size of a saddle-dogs.

Truth is, there have only been a few confirmed sightings of Bull Rabbit. Those who've actually seen him don't have any pictures, recordings, or corroborating witnesses; they only have the scars to prove it. Dale had the scars to prove he actually came face-to-face with Bull Rabbit!

I'd never heard Dale tell the story to anyone other than us boys. But one morning, the same year Ronny married Barb Bianchi, I was enjoying breakfast at The Manhole and got to be "just another listener" as Dale told his story…

A group of us scooted around the corner booth, one after the other. I was forced to sit next to Sheriff Beitzel as I was the last to shuffle in. Outside of the corner window, I watched four young women in thick-cotton dresses hand out Golden Highgrass flowers as they greeted patrons entering The Manhole.

"Would you like to learn about the People's Awakening of Ishmaelians?" they asked while handing out colorful flowers.

Dale startled me from my gaze as he quickly brushed a few crumbs from our table.

"I can remember my mother singing me the song of Bull Bunny every night while tucking me into bed," he reminisced while shaking the crumbs out of his damp white cloth and letting them disappear into the carpeted floor.

Dale sang, swaying his head back and forth while imitating his mother's voice,

> *"Big bull bunny, funny silly bunny,*
> *with your white fluffy tummy.*
> *Big bull bunny, funny silly bunny,*
> *protector of the forest, always there for us.*

"You ever wondered where the saying, 'Ay Chihuahua' comes from?" Dale asked as he filled our glasses with water. "My Great Grampa Gropes told me that long ago, Bull Rabbit was referred to as Chee-Wa-Wa. The large rabbit was believed to be the collected spirits of ancient native chiefs. Chee-Wa-Wa protected the forest and the people of the lands.

"Grampa Gropes taught me that if you're walking through the forest on a hot summer's day and suddenly feel cold air, it means Chee-Wa-Wa is near. And when Chee-Wa-Wa is close, you don't move! You stand still, be quiet, and wait for the cool air to pass. That's when you know Chee-Wa-Wa has moved on.

"But, if you ever find yourself in some kinda trouble in the forest, if you're injured or something; town elders say to yell, '*Ouch Chee-Wa-Wa,*' and the giant rabbit will come to your rescue.

"Like many phrases and sayings, over time, Ouch Chee-Wa-Wa became bastardized and misused. Folks began using the phrase as slang for moments of frustration.

"You run outta gas, *Ouch Chee-Wa-Wa.* You break a coffee cup, *Ouch Chee-Wa-Wa.* You squeeze a bottle of ketchup and get nothing but ketchup water, *Ouch Chee-Wa-Wa.* Over years of misuse, 'Ouch Chee-Wa-Wa' slowly became shortened to 'Ay Chihuahua.'

"Anyways…" Dale smiled and put his hands on his hips. "That's just a little backstory for ya," he chuckled and placed menus on the table as the early morning diner hummed in the background.

"Years ago, when I was just a boy, I was walking through the woods on the edge of Redman's farm heading west toward Mumper. I decided to take a shortcut; feeling confident that I could find my way. I figured I could follow the creek to keep my bearings. After a while, I needed a little break. So, I walked up the embankment where the blackberries grow. But the bank was so steep that I had to stop halfway up to catch my breath.

"As I was catching my breath, I looked down at the creek and saw a bay-breasted warbler perched on a twig. I'd never seen a bay-breasted warbler before. I stood there and watched it drink from the creek for several minutes before it flew off into the forest. That's when I noticed the Ferris Wheel Chapel in the distance."

"There ain't no points high enough on Redman's farm to see the Ferris Wheel Chapel," Miss Poterspeel snarked from her booth across the aisle.

"Doggone Gray-Haired Goose," Sheriff Beitzel mumbled while biting into a sausage patty smooshed between glazed donuts.

"Ain't dat da trute," Shiffy loudly agreed.

"Shut it, Shiffy," the sheriff yelped, coughing out mushy donut chunks onto the table. "Don't get that sack 'a bones started."

Miss Poterspeel was about the unfriendliest person in town. Heck, she was so nasty that she made grumpy old Redman seem like a church camp counselor. To be fair, she'd never been quite right in the head after her "flying-with-the-geese" incident back when the boys and I were kids.

Every August first, Stoolmist has its annual geriatric water-skiing competition called Old Mold on the Lake. Miss Poterspeel, in her gray onesie and black swim cap, was cutting in on her skis when the wake of another boat hit her blind side and sent the old lady flying through the air.

While she soared above the water, a flock of passing geese formed a flying V behind her. The spectators on shore *oohed* and *aahed,* bursting into cheer as folks called out, "Look at that. Up in the sky... It's a gray-haired goose!"

The fella commentating over the loud speakers announced, "Looks like that old bird can still fly!"

As elegant as Miss Poterspeel looked in the air, her landing was less than graceful. She hit the water like a doctor's hand on a newborn's butt, *smack!*

Miss Poterspeel got her five-minutes of fame after a photograph of her flying through the air, with geese flanked on either side, was printed on the front page of *The Stoolmist Post.* The headline read,

> *"Look out Loch Ness Monster, the Gray-Haired Goose Flies the Skies of the Dustfog Region!"*

"Ding dang doggone it, Shiffy," Sheriff Beitzel screamed as he pointed to the mushy donut chunks he spat on the table. "You payin' for that Shiffy! I ain't payin' full price for half eaten food damn it!"

"Oh, my word… Sheriff," Miss Poterspeel gasped. "Profanity in public? I would never."

The old lady continued mumbling to herself while gathering her things to leave when Marie-Agnus brought our attention back to Dale's story.

"Y'all seen inside Preacher Jepp's house cart on the Ferris Wheel Chapel?" Marie-Agnus asked. "It's beautiful. It's just as nice as Jytis's tiny house in dumpster #4 at the trash yard behind the Neff's home."

"Preacher Jepp had an Ormish man shingle the sides, install windows and build a fold-out roof. It's basically water proof. He installed wood floors, a hammock bed, and little shelves. It's sooo cozy," she blushed while stirring her tea and gazing out the window; seemingly lost in a dream.

"One evening, Preacher Jepp invited me over for a private bible study, and to taste test a bottle of pumpkin wine he bought while visiting Mumper. He rotated the Ferris Wheel so we were sitting at the highest point and took the top off of his tiny cart. The two of us just stared at the stars all night until the sun came up. It was such a beautiful moment."

"That ain't the only *top that came off* from what I hear," Miss Poterspeel muttered.

The sheriff interrupted, "Okay, okay, enough of the kissy wissy stuff. Go on with the story Dale. You was lost… waren't ya?"

"Yes sir," Dale replied. "Miss Poterspeel is right. You can't see the Ferris Wheel Chapel from Redman's farm. That's when I knew I was lost.

"I decided to keep walking up the creek bank for a better view. When I turned to step up the hill, my foot got caught, and I fell back with an unexpected force," Dale smacked his hands together with a *crack,* startling Marie-Agnus and Barb.

"I don't know how long I was knocked out. It was probably only a few minutes, but it felt like an eternity. When I came to, my vision was blurry, and my ears were ringing a high-pitched tone as the sun shined through a small opening in the trees, burning my glazed eyes. I felt the blood rushing to my head as I lay on my back, upside down, sloping downhill.

"Slowly, I lifted my head and saw my right shoe lace tangled on a tree root. I tried sitting up to release it, but I didn't have the strength. The slightest movement was agonizing. I was afraid. I was injured. I was stuck!

"I laid helpless as I began feeling the pain of my injury. I reached back and felt my hair wet with blood. I shut my eyes to ease my throbbing head.

The breeze whistling through the trees sounded like waves gently rolling onto the shore. I tried to yell for help, but nothing came out of my mouth; for my cries were in the silence of my own mind.

"I could feel the Earth spin beneath me as my silent screams for help mirrored the rhythm of my throbbing skull, which strangely comforted me in my despair. I floated in and out of consciousness, and then, I began to hear the voice of my Great Grampa Gropes. *'Ouch Chee-Wa-Wa,'* over and over, like a song sung with the sound of the breeze."

Dale closed his eyes as those of us listening around the booth sat with bated breath.

"Ouch Chee-Wa-Wa, Ouch Chee Wa-Wa...

"As the melody eased my pain, I saw the sunlight shining through my eyelids go dark, as if someone, or something, was standing over me.

"The air grew cold as I shivered in the shadow of the umbra of death. I had nothing left... I laid there in surrender, accepting my fate. In the end, my eyes were shut when the darkness came."

Dale wasn't lost; he was confused. He thought he was walking west toward Mumper, but was actually walking south toward Chigger Bottom. If not for falling, eventually he would've seen the flags of Dust Fog Market in the distance and realized his mistake.

If you head south out of Big Rug and pass through Dust Fog Market, you'll find a soft stone brook called Green Wind Stream. The creek Dale was following through Redman's farm connects with Green Wind Stream, which flows south through Chigger Bottom.

Dale has been squirrel hunting in the forests of Chigger Bottom since he was old enough to ride-the-saddle. Heck... Dale was the one who took me on my first squirrel hunt. And he took me to Chigger Bottom! So, like I said, Dale wasn't lost... he was confused.

Chigger Bottom is a beautiful part of the Dustfog Region. The weeping willows lining Green Wind Stream reach down, letting their leaves dance on the water like tinsel glistening in the sun.

In the summer, the boys and I would watch the minnows disappear in the ripples of the dancing leaves. Frogs would plop into the water as birds chirped songs in the pockets of sunlight.

By the water's edge, it's shaded and cool with thick green grass where spotted box turtles hide. And, it's the only forest in the region that inhabits bay-breasted warblers. The same bay-breasted warbler Dale saw before tripping and hitting his head.

In the fall, Green Wind Stream becomes a long thin mushy marsh with a bed of leaves soaked in mud. By December, the colorful splendor of the stream is bleached by the blanketing snow. White on white; erasing all edges. Out there in the forest, the silence of a damp winter's day is so mute, you can hear your pulse pumping in your ears.

In the spring, Green Wind Stream grows thick with water dipping and curling as the snow melts off the high ground. There's a spot under a weeping willow on Boulder Corner where the stream widens into a reflection pond.

I used to sit under the willow tree as a boy and play my harmonica when I needed time alone. The water reflected the leaves, and the leaves reflected the water; like a kaleidoscope of twinkling realities in a shimmering dome of tranquility.

As the water at Boulder Corner shallows in the dry season, its large sandstone bottom becomes visible. On one stone, someone carved two sentences that can only be seen when the water runs low.

"What you desire, can only be found from within.
For the happiness you seek, you already possess."

In the dusk of summer, I'd sit under that weeping willow on Boulder Corner, and read those two lines as lightning bugs rose from the creek bank.

"What does it mean?" I asked.

"It means a couple of dopey-dopes vandalized a rock with gibberish," my father replied.

"I think it's biblical," Mama said. "Like, a lost scroll from the ministry of Yoder or something…"

"Like I said," Pops insisted, "A couple of dopey-dopes."

I suppose it's possible some kids carved it in the stone as an act of youthful rebellion. But it was carved so neatly, so precisely; some might say, elegantly. Not like what you'd expect from a couple dopey-dopes vandalizing a rock. This was well done. Like the sign at Don't Drink Paint Supply that Pucker Loaf—the best dang artist on Earth—hand painted.

"What you desire, can only be found from within. For the happiness you seek, you already possess."

A message from someone in another time, separate from the world I knew back then, and the world I know now.

I'd sit and look at the carving while daydreaming about what the brook used to be before I was alive and what it would be after I die. How many people had sat where I sat, discovered what I discovered? How many will sit after me? Who else will enjoy the stream while resting under a willow tree?

I haven't been back to Boulder Corner since I was a kid. But every time I think about Dale slipping in and out of consciousness on that creek bank, I think about those two sentences carved in the sandstone; and for a moment, I'm transported back to a simpler time… Back to my shimmering dome of tranquility.

"My eyes were shut when the darkness came," Dale continued, lowering his head from the weight of the memory.

"I believed that whatever was standing above me—blocking the sunlight and bringing the darkness—was nothing more than my mind fading away as I slowly died. I was in bad shape… My breath grew shallower and shallower as a chill shivered through my spine."

Dale paused to manage his emotions and took a deep breath.

"I've heard stories of injured hikers feeling cold moments before entering the gates of heaven," Barb spoke softly. "Even in the heat of summer they feel cold. Maybe from blood loss or something? I don't know… It all just sounds scary to me."

"Uncle Willard died from too many wives," Sheriff Beitzel blurted out with a mouth full of hash browns.

"And…" he coughed, clearing his throat while doing a little shimmy to get comfortable in the booth, "all 'a them wives said Uncle Willard had a cold heart."

"Ain't dat da trute," Shiffy mumbled.

"Shut it, Shiffy," the sheriff snapped. "Uncle Willard was a saint! They's talkin' 'bout the cold…'n dyin' in the cold! From the frosty bites, 'n the different heart bloods, 'n the…'n the…'n yous don't even know what it is, dang it!"

The sheriff wiped the sweat from his forehead and began aggressively cutting into his pancakes.

"Sooo…what happened next?" Marie-Agnus asked looking confused by the sheriff's rambling.

"With my last breath, and last bit of strength, I opened my eyes. The sunlight flickered through the leaves like a rolling wave cleansing my soul. The forest had never sounded so calm. At first, I thought my ears were ringing, drowning out all other sounds. But there was no ringing. There were no sounds. Only a vacuum of silence; so foreign, and so strange, that it snapped me into a brief moment of clarity.

"The shadow above me had passed. I turned my head to a large, dark silhouette on top of the creek bank near my foot. I squinted to bring the dark object into focus, and that's when I saw him… That's when I saw Bull Rabbit!"

There was a collective gasp amongst us sitting in the booth. Even the Gray-Haired Goose was leaning in at this point.

"He was sitting atop the hill gazing down at me… A giant!" Dale shouted and jumped from his chair. "His broad fluffy ears blocked the sunlight like oversized oven mitts. His whiskers were thick as spaghetti pasta and the length of a yard stick. His eyes…"

Dale slid back into his chair, shaking his head in astonishment.

"His eyes looked like black shiny billiard balls as he stared at me, chewing on a large stalk of shadecane.

"And then…from the forest canopy above, a bright red cardinal glided down and landed on Bull Rabbit's back."

Our eyes followed as Dale floated his open hand in front of him in a swooping motion down to the table.

"The bird's feet and belly disappeared in Bull Rabbit's thick hair. The size of the rabbit dwarfed the cardinal. It perched on Bull Rabbit's back, as if to say, *Now you see who is king of the forest!*

"The image of that cardinal standing on Bull Rabbit's back was so powerful, and so magnificent, that I became overwhelmed by its awesomeness and slipped back into unconsciousness."

Dale paused and rubbed his brow in a moment of post-traumatic stress. He refilled Sheriff Beitzel's chocolate milk before continuing to recount the events of that day.

"When I woke, I heard folks calling my name in the distance as the long shadows of dusk draped over me. I wasn't dangling at the top of the creek bank anymore. I'd rolled down to the water's edge and was lying in a patch of shadecane. The ground was cool and soft, cushioned by the moist soil and large yellow leaves. I felt...comfortable...and somehow safe.

"My right shoe lace had been chewed apart. Bull Rabbit freed me!" Dale proclaimed as tears glazed his brown eyes. "Bull Rabbit saved my life!"

"Bull Rabbit heard the chant!" Marie-Agnus put her hand to her chest. "The chant in your head. He heard it—or sensed it or something—and then saved you!"

"I believe so," Dale whispered and gently touched Marie-Agnus's hand with his.

"Punch a monkey's uncle," Sheriff Beitzel said.

Dale laughed a little and added, "The great Chee-Wa-Wa has powers that no one can understand. Powers that live in the folklore of the Dustfog Region."

"The Ormish say these lands are magic," Barb commented, triggering Sheriff Beitzel to pop up and rattle the booth.

"Met a magic Ormish fella fishin' out at Lake Sippo once," the Sheriff interrupted. "Put a penny in his nose...pulled it outta my ear!

I knocked that feller right in the shin with my sheriff stick! Lucky I didn't lock him up for witchcraft," he blabbed, spilling a few drinks from rattling the table with his knee as he crossed his legs.

My friends," Dale wiped the table dry, "as sure as I'm standing here today, I saw Bull Rabbit! And I have the scar to prove it."

Dale slowly turned his back to us and lifted his hair, exposing a scar on the back of his head from the root knot he cracked his noggin on. He then lifted his hand out above the center of the table for all of us to see. Wrapped around his wrist was the old chewed apart shoelace from that day. I heard the sheriff gulp loudly as the rest of us sat in shock.

"That's why you wear house slippers," Barb concluded putting two and two together. "You're afraid of shoelaces."

Dale nodded his head and affirmed, "Yes ma'am. I'll never get tangled up by a shoelace again… Never again!" he shouted.

"I remember that day," Sheriff Beitzel grunted while pouring syrup over a double plate of early bird brisket-biscuits. "Got a call a boy gone missin'."

"Yes," Miss Poterspeel nagged from across the aisle. "I remember too. All kinds went out lookin'. Caused a big commotion that day. Took me thirty minutes to check out of Thrifty Foods. But I don't remember you searching for the boy, Sheriff."

The sheriff slammed his silverware on the table.

"I almost died that day too damn it! Got the call and went to change outta my town britches in to my brush britches. In the chaos I forgot to take my shoes off. I was trouser trapped," he screamed and pointed at Miss Poterspeel.

"You ever get your britches flipped inside out, and wrapped around your shoes? Trouser Trappins ain't no joke! Old folks, just like you Miss Poterspeel, die…every day…from a trouser trappin'!

"I laid there alone in my office. No food… No water… All day 'n night with nothing but floor food to survive on. No toilet," the fat man huffed and puffed. "Thank the good lord my office has absorbent carpet…or there would've been a real mess to clean up when Shiffy found me the next morning."

Shiffy quietly mouthed, "Ain't dat da trute."

"Shut it, Shiffy!" Sheriff Beitzel whined. "I was trouser trapped damn it," he pleaded to us. "Trouser trapped!"

In the summer of eighth grade, there was a thin-stached bucktooth workin' the ticket line at the mud slide behind the town's communal shower station.

"Shower in the suds, slide in the muds," he announced while tearing off tickets.

That thin-stache was obsessed with Bull Rabbit! Dale was like a celebrity to that pimple popper. He let us boys slide in the mud for free all summer! So, like I said at the beginning…the day Dale graced the cover of the *Big Rug Repository* was the day that everything changed for us boys.

If the newspaper had never written a story about Dale's encounter with Bull Rabbit, we would've never spent that summer mud slidin'. At least, I wouldn't have… I wasn't about to pay ten cents to slide down the mud hill where the water drains out behind the communal shower. Free, I'll do; ten cents, I will not…

I mean, yeah, it was a nice size hill… And the soapy shower water mixed with the mud let you pick up some serious speed. But ten cents is outrageous!

Heck, one time, I heard my Uncle Shty tell Pops that in Plumpstin City, folks let ladies roll around in the mud for free… Them gals don't pay not 'a penny! In fact, folks pay *them* to wrestle around in the mud. Talk about a dream job…

Lots of folks like that thin-stached buck-tooth fella are fascinated by Bull Rabbit. There are songs, books, memorabilia, clubs, and just about anything else you can think of to honor—or cash in on—the mythical creature. So, it's no surprise that the most popular tourist spot in town is Pucker Loaf's double-dumpster mural of Bull Rabbit in the parking lot of the Big Rug Town Hall and Drive-Through Deli.

Several people recognize Pucker Loaf as the greatest living artist in the world. And what his artistic mind created in honor of Bull Rabbit is simply exquisite…

Two dumpsters; side-by-side. On one, a beautifully-painted image of Bull Rabbit standing at the edge of a forest trail with a little bright red cardinal perched on his back. On the other, an excerpt from Truce Deradodo's journal that reads:

> *"And as I walked through the crisp cool breeze;*
> > *a rabbit stood, as tall as me.*
> *Bumble bees buzzed, circling left to right;*
> > *a buzzing pollen halo, crowned his head with light.*
> *I fell to my knees, overwhelmed by the sight;*
> > *the king of the forest, in the day and the night."*

Pucker painted the whole thing free hand! No tracing or stencils…

Brekanny and I had our engagement party at the double dumpsters. It was actually a lovely venue, for a parking lot. The dumpster's smelled pretty bad though.

But…my grampy warned me on the day I took the love walk to propose to Brekanny that, "Marriage stinks." So, the foul aroma at our engagement party didn't surprise me none.

In my opinion, the double dumpster mural of Bull Rabbit is the most impressive piece of art in town. Even more impressive than the skunk weasel sculpture at the Big Rug Magazine Library and Coupon Trading Post.

Heck… You'd be hard pressed to find any art, anywhere, more splendid than Pucker Loaf's double dumpsters.

I mean…I've personally never seen, but I've heard great things about Leonardo da Vinci's famous work of erotica, *The Moaning Lisa*…and I'm sure the dumpsters are just as sensual.

The game we play is not won one way.

— Yoderian proverb

THE BIG RUG
BOWLING BALL DISASTER

Chad had a nickname, The Navy Blue! He was all about that H2O!

"Make the bet, and I'll get wet," Chad would say as kids made wagers on who could beat him in a swimming race. No one ever did though. That boy was faster than a creek-dolphin swimming downstream in a snowmelt runoff!

I've never understood the saying, but when Chad was in water, he was "happy as a pig in poop." Or in Chad's case... I guess... a *dolphin* in poop?

One time, I overheard Chad's mother say that she was pretty sure Chad was "conceived" at the Tire Tube River Float event down in Chigger Bottom.

"Remember Roy Cob," she asked my mother.

"The guy with the tattoo of a lightning bolt frozen in a block of ice?" Mama sighed in disappointment.

"Yeppers… That's him," she blushed. "I shared an innertube with him during the float… And, well, it was a long float… So I was like, if they can't see, it's fine with me."

"And Roy knew all these facts and tratistics—"

"You mean statistics Darcey-Dee…" Mama interjected.

"Tratistics about electricity and wiring car radios," Chad's mom continued. "I'm pretty sure that's why Chady likes the water so much. Because he was conceived in water."

To this day, I have no idea what Chad's mother was talkin' 'bout… I "conceive" things all the time, but that don't make the things in my head real.

You know them blankets with sleeves that folks wear to the early morning services of church? I think they're called Snuggies? Well, one time I "conceived" of a more *sensual* Snuggie made with lace and other sexy-lady lingerie materials. I called it the Sluttie.

Aunt Sara made a prototype out of an old fishnet she found snagged at the bottom of Lake Sippo. It totally looked sensual! Smelled terrible though… No matter how many times we bleached it, it still smelled fishy. So, we gave up on the idea.

"If at first you don't succeed," Aunt Sara said while tossing our Sluttie prototype into the fire, "Give up! Because a second failure is almost guaranteed."

And, once you've seen your aunt in a Sluttie, you never see her the same way again. I should've had my mother-in-law be my garment tester. She died later that year, so the awkwardness wouldn't have lasted very long.

It's just like my grampy used to say, "If I knew then what I know now, I'd be eatin' horse and ridin' cow."

You ever seen all them rusted-out, broken-down trampolines folks have in their front yards? Well, one time I got to "conceiving" about all that wasted trampoline stretchy material and thought, *"Hey, why don't someone make jumpin' jeans outta that stuff? If you made them tight enough, when you bend down to jump, they'd probably spring you pretty high."*

I call them Tramp-O-Jeans!

Boof and I are working on the design. Boof keeps splitting the seams while attempting a "super jump." A term I coined for when a person jumps really high in their Tramp-O-Jeans. I conceived it, but I don't see no one struttin' 'round town in Slutties or Tramp-O-Jeans. Do you?

Anyway, there's no mystery about who Chad's father is; his name's Markio. He and Darcey-Dee had some kinda falling out before Chad was born, so he lived in a van in their backyard. I remember when Pops helped Markio put the van up on cinderblocks so no one could steal it. It was a nice van. Markio had a refrigerator in there and everything!

Ever seen the hair on a hefty gal's neck hump? It's thin, but typically has some length to it. Chad's head hair was just like a hefty gal's neck hump hair when we were kids. In the sunlight, it was like his hair would disappear, revealing the silhouette of a shiny head covered in long blond fuzz.

Chad's hair began receding at birth, like all the CaLaruzzo men in his family. Chad, like his father, and his father's father, were completely bald by the sixth grade.

You see, Chad had something in common with Ronny; a family lineage of historical relevance. Back when Truce Deradodo discovered the forested valley that's now Big Rug, he found natives living on the land. There's a passage in Truce's journal that reads:

> *"Three-quarter a fortnight, I severely sprained my ankle whilst going from seated to standing. I laid in solitude, unable to walk for days. I crawled, but became tangled in thorns and brush, losing my britches in the entanglement. I fear the Deradodo Clumsy Curse has followed me to this new land.*
>
> *"Oh, how I worried I might never see my beloved Blanch again. But alas, a small group of natives found me. Dehydrated, injured, and britchesless, I was in need, and the Lord answered my call.*
>
> *"The men and young boys were bald. Not a hair to their head. They claimed to be sons of a biblical bloodline marked by a lack of hair on their head. A holy lineage of the Hebrew prophet Elisha, who dawned the mark of the bald.*
>
> *"Elisha's father, Shaphat, also dawned the mark of the bald; and Shaphat's father, Adlai, was bald too. Logic tells me that these natives, who have saved me from certain death, must be descendants from the same biblical bloodline; for they too are bald. They shall be cherished members of the community I hope to build."*

So, if you're bald in the town of Big Rug, it's assumed that you're part of the same biblical bloodline as the indigenous people of this land. It's science!

Grampy once told me, "Ladies brush their hair, but real men have nothing to brush."

Some fellas in town fake being bald by shaving their heads to look more attractive. It looks good, but it just isn't the same.

Chad's father used to speak at the Big Rug Rotary Club once a year about *the power of the bald.* It was part of his duties as the president of the Big Rug "RIB" Club; *Responsibility in Baldness.* Every year, Pops made us go watch Markio give his speech.

"Free admission is free entertainment," Pops would say.

"Baldness, in the hands of the weak, can lead to a life of orgasmic vanity," is how Markio always began his speech. "These pleasures can pull a man into the depths of self-destruction. The power of the bald must be governed with responsibility. Most men can manage power with care, but if you want to test a man's character, let him do it without hair."

Us boys were first-hand witnesses to the follicle faculties of the bald while growing up with Chad. Baldness gave him liberties the rest of us boys could only dream of. Everyone treated the bald with respect back then. Even more than they do today. And today, if you're bald in Big Rug, you get early admission to all sporting events. So, yeah…being bald is a pretty big deal.

In the spring of tenth grade, Don't Drink Paint Supply was vandalized in an appalling defacement of private property. The paint store offers all five types of lacquer and almost twenty colors of paint and stain… What type of savage would harm such a place?

The paint store is attached to the Big Rug High School and Brush Burn Yard. At one point, they were separate buildings, until Principal Keck converted the empty lot between the two buildings into the school cafeteria.

The owners of Don't Drink Paint Supply agreed to pay half the cost to build the cafeteria if they could use part of it for storage. The paint fumes were always pretty thick in the cafeteria... Someone threw up pretty much every day from the toxic air... But Lunch Lady Irwin's Coney Bologna Pizza Thursday made it all worth it.

To add insult to injury, the vandals burnt "Ass Weasels" in the grass with gasoline. A slander directed at Big Rug's beloved mascot, the Mighty Skunk Weasel. Clearly, this was an act of war!

Stoolmist borders Big Rug to the north and has a long list of awful things about it. One of those awful things—a constant stain on the fabric of my childhood—was a group of slime-snotters the boys and I referred to as the Ferry Flowers of Stoolmist; Lincoln, Oliver, Hudson, and their leader—the golden-haired butt-weed—Preston. And the defacement of Don't Drink Paint Supply had their fingerprints all over it.

Those nerd-squirts caused more problems for us boys than I care to remember. One time, Fat Neck Oliver cut me in line at the pumpkin fries stand during Fall Fest. When I told the pumpkin fries lady that Fat Neck cut in line, he screamed, "You don't know jack squat," grabbed his fries, walked to the condiments stand, and took the last few squirts of balsamic mustard... What kinda horn-honker does something like that?

Standing beside the Ferry Flowers, more times than not, were the Three Blind Bats: Isabella, Ava, and Sofia. Them gals had to be "blind as a bat" to hang out with those ugly mugs.

The Ferry Flowers were so ugly they made catfish look like rainbow trout. Their stupid teeth were so straight, and so white, they looked like donkeys with show-horse teeth. And their hair was so shiny that it looked like a muff-cow was napping on their heads.

Preston was the biggest dunkaroo of them all. The kinda guy who never "rode-the-saddle" if you know what I mean... Probably had two or three saddle-dogs, but never rode 'a one.

He was tough though. I'll give him that. Broad shoulders like only swimmers get, sun bleached hair like only lake kids get, and a healthy gumline like only butt-wipes from Stoolmist get.

Back when Hank Deradodo was excavating the land for the Clown's Don't Frown Culinary Arts Institute, he uncovered a rare archeological find; bones that traced back to between 65 million and 230 million years ago. From a time known as the Mesozoic Era.

Muhck knows a thing or two when it comes to the prehistoric critters of the Dustfog Region! One time, I heard him bickering with Coach about who knew more about prehistoric critters.

"See na see, I knows the rock rats, jumpin' land-eels, pouch pigs, swamp oxen, ginger bugs," Muhck raddled off. "Short haired pond lobsters, leaf-goats, I knows 'em, see na see!"

"Big city gots prehistorics," Coach argued. "They live in alleyway dumpsters and breed in cardboard boxes. You know 'em when you see 'em.

"The gals got beards and the boys boast boobs. Push poo on the sidewalks and urinate in flowerpots. Seem harmless though... Big city prehistorics volunteer as security guards in the bathrooms. Watchin' folks. Keepin' a close eye on things."

Big Rugian culture is heavily influenced by its Jurassic past. It's the reason why Dr. Plakas named his ENT clinic Mesozoic Ear-a; and why the Big Rug junk yard is named Tyrannosaurus-Wrecks & Scrapodon Yard.

Heck, even Aunt Sara used the town's Jurassic past while advertising her one-hundred percent, genuine cat hair blouses. She took out an ad in the *Big Rug Repository* that read, *"Try-Sara's-Tops,"* with a picture of her golden retriever wearing two fake horns on his head, and one on his nose. The dog actually resembled a triceratops if you ask me.

Cat hair really is a luxurious material. Aunt Sara sews all of my athletic socks with Persian cat hair; the "most absorbent" of the feline furs. Sometimes, my ankles break out in hives, but like Mama says, "That's the price you pay for fashion!"

Scientists divide the Mesozoic Era into three periods: the Triassic, Jurassic, and Cretaceous periods. During the Cretaceous period, there was a stinky critter native to the lands of Big Rug. A beautiful blend of skunk and weasel, called the Pink Stink Weasel.

Named after its hairless ass and bright pink skin, the pink stink weasel is recognized by local historians as one of the most odorous mammals to ever live. The stinky prehistoric scavenger is commonly referred to as the skunk weasel!

Unlike the common skunk, which has two glands on each side of its keister for spraying potential predators, the skunk weasel omitted a continuous odor from its pores. A full-body stench. An odor so heavy, it would've made your ears ring.

Muhck said that it would've been near impossible to avoid the stink of a skunk weasel.

"See na see, the skunk weasel was the king of the critters back then. Nasty little critter! Dirty little critter," Muhck said while flipping the back of his mullet. "Clever critters though... Type of critter that you might catch, but not before they catch you first! Catch you with the stinky stink!"

The skunk weasel is so inspirational to Big Rugians that Pucker Loaf sculpted an oversized replica of the majestic creature and donated it to the Big Rug Magazine Library and Coupon Trading Post. Once a year the librarian scrapes the slime out of his compost bucket and sets it in a cheesecloth sack next to the sculpture for an "immersive viewing experience." Boof threw up the first time Pops took the family. She got a free pencil for adding to the smell.

A cartoon version of the skunk weasel serves as our school mascot and is the most requested tattoo in town. So, like I said, when them rash wrinkles up in Stoolmist burnt "Ass Weasels" into the grass at Don't Drink Paint Supply, it was an act of war that couldn't be ignored. So, it's just like my grampy used to say, "Best return the favor, if another's favor harmed your neighbor."

Nuff said!

Gus had the idea, I had the car, Mitch had the attitude, and Chad had an I.Q. low enough to make the whole thing a memory worth remembering.

"Chad, if you can swipe your dad's bowling ball, and Tuck," Gus turned his head so fast his double chin wobbled like a slice of chilled gravy pie, "if you can borrow your Uncle Shty's car, I can toss the bowling ball out the window. It'll bounce up the sidewalk of the Stoolmist Indoor Pool with enough speed that it'll burst through the brick on its way in," he said punching his right hand forward. *And*...it'll roll through the building and burst through the brick on its way out," he punched his left hand forward. "Them Ferry Flowers won't know what hit 'em!"

"Genius," I smirked.

"Oh wait… There's more," Gus replied. "One of us can crawl through the hole and put green food coloring in the pool. It'll look like a sewer pit or something."

"Gross," we laughed at the image of those Stoolmist dork-corks walking in and seeing green water in their pool.

"Who's going to squeeze through the hole?" Mitch asked, grabbing the white stick of the little round lollipop in his mouth and chomping down with a *crunch*.

Mitch was a health nut, but he had a sweet tooth. So he was usually sucking on a cherry-red lollipop. The white sucker stick pocking out of his mouth complimented his slicked back hair and black leather jacket quite well.

"Big Gut Gus isn't squeezing through anything smaller than a barn door," Mitch joked.

To which Gus replied, "Well, Lord knows you ain't doing anything that might ruffle your manicured hair. How many tubs of lard does it take to grease back your hair anyway? You look like a water-resistant alpaca who's part of some hipster motorbike club."

Chad stood up, interrupting Gus and Mitch's bickering; his bald head glistening in the sunlight as he spoke, "Make the bet…and I'll get wet!"

And just like that, the Big Rug Bowling Ball Disaster began!

Chad ran home and got his dad's bowling ball while Gus raided his mom's kitchen cabinets for green food coloring. Mitch and I headed over to Uncle Shty's lawnmower shop to cash in on a favor he owed me.

A few weeks earlier, I walked in my house and found Coach and Uncle Shty in my mother's closet trying on her shirts while flexing in the mirror.

"Big city stuff," I heard Coach's voice coming from my parent's bedroom. "All the city boys in the city wear tight lady's shirts to show off their muscles.," he was explaining as I opened the bedroom door.

Uncle Shty shrugged and questioned, "I don't know Coach man… My pit hair stickin' outta these little lady sleeves… Shirt's so tight I can see my bellybutton."

"That's how it's s'pposed to be," Coach reassured him.

Mama came home shortly after their little fashion show and found her t-shirts stretched loose as an old lady's elbow skin. When she burst into the bathroom—where we were hiding—she found Coach stuck in the window from a failed escape, Uncle Shty pretending to be sleep walking, and me washing my hands as if nothing was going on at all.

"Oh…what da? Where am I?" Uncle Shty stuttered, pretending to be waking up from his sleep walk.

I ended up telling Mama that I was the one who stretched out her shirts. I said my saddle-dog, Gamb-Balls, was getting bit by mosquitos, and I thought putting a shirt on him would help.

So, Uncle Shty owed me a favor for taking the blame. And that favor was borrowing his old teal Chevy. He handed me the keys, and our journey began.

Mitch and I picked up Chad, with his father's bowling ball in hand, and then Gus, who had little bottles of green food coloring falling out of his letterman's jacket as he ran to the car.

"Let's shake a leg," Gus giggled as he plopped his round body into the passenger seat.

We rolled down the windows and began the thirty-minute drive up to Stoolmist, energized by the crescent moon floating in the cool spring sky.

"Get 'er up to fifty-five," Gus shouted as we approached the Stoolmist Indoor Pool.

I could hear Chad and Mitch chanting "Go—Go—Go," from the back seat as I gripped the wheel and pressed the gas.

"On my command, pull the emergency break," Gus hollered while hanging halfway out of the passenger side window with the purple bowling ball on his shoulder.

"Faster," he yelled.

The nausea in my stomach grew as the headlights lit up the brick building in the distance.

"Faster…"

The adrenaline-rich blood pulsed through my veins.

"Get ready…"

Gus shimmied his fat body into position.

"Pull it!" he howled into the night sky.

I jerked the emergency break, causing the tires to lock-up and squeal like a donkey stepping on a prickle-patch. The back end of the old Chevy turned left to right in its skid, catapulting the bowling ball out from Gus's hands and toward the brick building.

The four of us watched the purple ball tumble down the sidewalk through the smoke of the tires, skipping and jumping in the direction of its target. The ball leapt into the air and burst through the building; leaving a surprisingly clean hole in the brick about the size of a fat man's thigh.

"Beef cigar!" Gus celebrated as we exploded into cheers.

I couldn't believe it worked. Everything went just how Gus predicted. We cheered while jumping out of the car to admire our greatest life accomplishment. But our cheers soon turned to jeers as the Big Rug Bowling Ball Disaster reared its ugly head.

When we ran to the back of the building, there was no exit hole, and no bowling ball. In Gus's copious calculations, he failed to take into account that once the ball entered the building, it wouldn't roll to the other side…because of the F-ing pool!

"What happened?" Big Gut Gus asked, gasping for air while running up to Chad.

Chad, in a state of shock and unable to respond, snapped back into attention after a good smack to his shoulder from Gus.

"Holy pickle pinch fella's," he said white as a ghost. "My dad's name is on that ball. I'm shit up creek without a paddle."

Chad's choice of words triggered an immediate meltdown by Mitch. I watched Mitch's eye twitch as his brain literally broke.

"Chad… You dunce! How do you forget your dad's name is on the ball," he shouted, popping the collar of his black leather jacket and spinning toward Gus. "And I should've known better than to follow a plan concocted by you Gus! You still owe me a nickel from investing in your stupid turtle race idea."

"The turtle races *were* a good idea," Gus contended. "It didn't work—*Mitch*—because the economy is 'a bust.'"

Mitch waved his arms and wailed, "It's boring… No one will pay to watch turtles race. I got zero return on my investment! All I did was donate six turtles to the pond."

He turned back to Chad while putting his hands to his hips.

"And…Chad…that's not even how the saying goes! Are you suggesting *we* are pieces of shit…? Pieces of shit…up a creek…without a paddle? How does that make any sense? Are we pieces of shit Chad?" Mitch asked condescendingly. "We're up *shit-creek*…without a paddle, Chad! That's the saying! Not *shit* up creek… Up *shit-creek!*"

"Shut your yappers," I barked, running around to the front of the building as the boys followed.

I imagined our fate come Monday morning when the Stoolmist faculty arrived to see a hole in their aquatic gymnasium, inevitably finding a bowling ball resting at the bottom of the pool with Chad's father's league name on it; Markio *'Balder than Bald'* CaLaruzzo.

"I'm dead as a door nail," Chad pouted hopelessly, slouching his shoulders in despair. "Mitch, can you get a cat to go through the hole and like...unlock the door or something?"

"I'm not a damn cat wizard," Mitch snapped back.

"Wiz-tard," Gus quietly laughed to himself.

"Cat's just follow me around," Mitch argued while waving his cherry-red lollipop in the air. "They don't listen to me like a saddle-dog or something. I can't control what they do. If I could, I wouldn't be hanging out with you losers doing stupid stuff like this! I'd start a cat circus and be rich!"

"Would you serve hot dogs?" Gus inquired with a serious tone. "Or would the cats be offended?"

"Maybe they could be called hotcats," Chad suggested. "No. Meatcats! No... Weinercats! Call 'em weinercats!"

"Do cats get offended?" Gus turned toward Mitch and casually bit into a fresh jerky stick while sitting Ormish-style in the grass. "I know cats are judgmental... They always stare at me in a judgmental way. And I know it's because they think I'm fat."

"It's true," Chad teased. "Everything you said is true,"

"Shut it, *Navy Poo!* I'm big boned," Gus demanded, holding up his thick wrist.

"What I'm saying is this," he continued and pointed his jerky stick at Mitch. "I'm not paying to go to a cat circus if they don't have a meat option at the concession stand. Popcorn is delicious, and Lord knows

I love a good ballpark pretzel. But that ain't a real meal! I need somethin' with meat and a bun! Protein and carbs; that's a real meal."

It was at that moment—during the discussion about the food options of a make-believe cat circus—that I actually began to panic. The reality of the situation smacked me in the face like a cold slice of ham. A thick slice too. The kind that'll really wake you up. Aunt Sara smacked me across the face with a cold slice of ham on my sixth birthday for taking two crescent rolls. She knocked me right outta my chair. My cheek was red for a week.

"Sheriff Shitzel's gonna throw us all in jail, and we're talkin' 'bout a cat circus," I scream-whispered at Gus.

Gus sighed and pulled down on his leather gloves.

"Okay, okay," he reassured me. "Don't wet the bed Tuck. Ya dang pool-party-pooper."

Gus pulled out a fresh jerky stick from his jacket pocket and pondered for a moment.

"I got it!" he declared. "We just stick to the original plan. Chad...we'll push you through the hole, you swim down, grab the ball, and we'll get outta here. No one will ever know it was us."

"Make the bet, and I'll get wet," Chad agreed.

We quietly, but frantically, helped Chad through the hole, doing our best to be on the lookout for headlights. He quickly stripped down to his birthday suit and jumped in the pool to retrieve the ball.

"Hurry up," I said nervously while looking over my shoulder for a passerby.

Chad swam up and pushed the bowling ball out of the pool with a smile ear to ear.

"Give me a minute," he whispered as we peered at him through the hole in the brick wall. "I'm a leave 'em a floater."

"What the heck are you talkin' 'bout? Let's go," Mitch demanded, nervously looking over his shoulder.

"I'm a leave 'em a pool oyster," Chad chimed.

"A what?" Mitch scolded while Gus and I laughed.

"A porcelain potato; a brown pickle; a rusty nugget," Chad rattled off while lifting his toes out of the water and wiggling them. "A fresh piece of squeezed fanny fudge…?"

Mitch was in a state of confusion as he gazed blankly at a naked Chad swimming carefree around the Stoolmist Indoor Pool in the middle of the night.

"What makes you so dumb Chad? Is it the inner ear infections from swimming so much?"

"A dumpy-doo…? A butt truffle…?" Chad swirled around the pool. "Pikachu de la poo-poo…? A sewer dog?"

Gus was laughing so hard he had to pull his shirt up to absorb his tears. Even a tough guy like Mitch would be hard pressed not to find humor in the situation.

"You're all a bunch of cornhusks," Mitch grinned. "Get outta the pool chrome dome!"

Chad swam to the edge, "Okay, okay…relax Mitch. Don't be such a *butt baby*."

"Yeah, Mitch," I teased through my laughter. "Don't be such a *keister log*.

The only thing Big Gut Gus could squeak out through his laughter was, *"Winnie the poo-poo"* in a high-pitched voice, erupting all four of us into laughter.

Chad scooped up his clothes, grabbed the bowling ball, and the four of us piled into the car and got the heck out of Stoolmist; celebrating our revenge on those sally-haired Ferry Flowers the whole way home.

But, yet again, the Big Rug Bowling Ball Disaster took us boys in an unforeseen direction that even Big Gut Gus couldn't have predicted.

The following evening, Shiffy and the sheriff showed up on Chad's doorstep with a pair of underwear in a wet paper bag. In all the commotion, no one—including Chad—noticed the missing article of clothing on the way home. But there was Sheriff Beitzel, holding a pair of tighty-whities with the words "The Navy Blue" written on the inside of the elastic band.

"These your under-britches son?" Sheriff Beitzel asked as Chad's mom covered her mouth in shock. "I almost drowned retrievin' these here undies."

"Ain't dat da trute!" Shiffy yelled, startling those within earshot.

"Ding dang doggone it!" Sheriff Beitzel squealed, placing his hand over his heart to try and calm his breathing. "We's standin' right here. Why you screamin' all the time... Talk normal dang it!

"And... you ever tried swimmin' with shoes on Shiffy?" he paused for a response. "Didn't think so. It ain't easy!"

Chad told the sheriff he acted alone. Everyone knew he was lying, but Chad refused to give us boys up. He said that he smashed the hole in the Stoolmist Indoor Pool while practicing his karate kicks. The only person who believed him was his mother.

"I've seen Chady karate kicking in the yard, and it's really impressive," she bragged while filing her nails.

The cigarette dangling between her lips bounced like a springboard with every word as she squinted from the burning tobacco smoke.

"I made him start practicing karate kicking back when the Tickle Monster was terrorizing the town. Remember...? The Huggabees went missing... I wasn't 'bout to let Chady die too.

"And everyone knows you can't keep Chady outta water. It's really the Stoolmist people's fault if you ask me… Who puts a pool inside? How do ya suntan?"

A few weeks after the Big Rug Bowling Ball Disaster, us boys got together for the *Friday night shoot 'em up cowboy western story* on the A.M. radio. We headed to the fire pit in the woods behind Beer Man Neff's house to roast marshmallows and enjoy the evening.

Mr. Neff was our high school history teacher and baseball coach. His folks owned Neffro's Big Batch Jerky & Taxadermy, so he always had tasty meats to munch on during class.

He kept a hidden icebox full of beer in the cellar behind his house because Mrs. Neff didn't "approve of the booze." The boys and I would occasionally steal some cold ones on our way to the fire pit; which is why we called him Beer Man Neff. He'd let us snatch a few brews as long as we didn't tell Mrs. Neff about his secret "beer box;" which he moronically had carved onto the lid of the box.

Things got complicated for Beer Man Neff during one of our baseball games when Mrs. Neff heard us chanting, "Here We Go Beer Man, Here We Go…*Beer Man!*"

In a moment of panic—and to protect the secrecy of his beloved booze—Mr. Neff told her that we were *not* chanting "Beer Man," but were *actually* chanting "Queer Man."

That's right… Mr. Neff so loved his suds, that he told his own wife he was secretly a stubble-rubber. To prove he was really a pinky-pointer, he started holding hands with our third base coach, Petey-Parv Pritchet, during games.

"A public display *proves* I'm gay!" he passionately announced to the stands while grabbing coach Pritchet's hand. "If you eat gum, you chew gum," he proclaimed, while lifting their clasped hands into the air as if they had just completed a marathon.

Petey-Parv and Mr. Neff have been best friends since childhood. Other than Mr. Neff, Petey-Parv doesn't have many friends—or much of a social life to speak of—on account of him being a, "Damn freeloading bum who couldn't sharpen an axe if his dinner were sittin' in a twig tree," as my father once described him. Drinking brews with Mr. Neff is about the only thing Petey-Parv has ever had going for him. So, he was happy to play along with Mr. Neff's stubble-rubber claim.

Several years later, I learned that Mrs. Neff knew the entire time that her husband wasn't a feather-foot with Petey-Parv Pritchet; and she knew about his secret beer box. She just played along with his shenanigans to punish him. For two years, Mr. Neff and Petey-Parv Pritchet held hands at our summer league baseball games while Mrs. Neff, and everyone else, laughed at them. You'd think the pinky-pointers around town would be offended by two guys pretending to be gaywads, but they enjoyed the show as much as everyone else.

Uncle Shty once told me, "It ain't a lie, if *parts* are true!" Mr. Neff may not have known how to hide booze from his wife, but he knew how to add truth to a lie. He and Petey-Parv went to some serious lengths trying to convince folks they were limp wrists. They drove to Plumpstin City the first Friday of every month for soft-shake classes at Dainty Shakes, *"Pour de belles rencontres."* You almost have to admire that kinda commitment to a lie.

"No matter what ya say, gotsta be born gay," is what Grampy told Boof and I.

It was pretty uncommon for folks to fake being a limp wrist back then. Beer Man and Petey-Parv were really swinging for the fences on that one. I mean, "faking the bald" by shaving your head is one thing, but to fake being a twinkle-dinkle…that's a stretch.

Heck, I'd say feather-foots are probably the most interesting folks around town! The majority of our town council members are pinky-pointers. Cheese on Cheese, Yes & Please, Brunch Bistro and Manners School is owned by a couple stubble-rubbers. Principle Keck bumps doughnuts with the bacon grease gal down at The Manhole. And my cousin Fannie is a limp wrist!

Fannie's a homo with a fella he met down at the Clowns Don't Frown Culinary Arts Institute. They share a necklace together. They trade-off wearing it week-to-week.

Back when Beer Man Neff was entangled in the "I'm gay" scandal, I overheard Mrs. Neff venting to my mother one night about the whole ordeal.

"Even after a year of classes at Dainty Shakes, those two morons still can't shake hands with sass. You know he got Petey-Parv to pay for the classes at Dainty Shakes so I wouldn't notice the missing money! I mean, they're idiots, right," she laughed while taking a sip of wine.

Mama sighed, "I've always wanted to take a class at Dainty Shakes. Feather-foots are just so elegant when they shake hands."

"I want to go to Dainty Shakes too," Mrs. Neff confessed.

"I mean, that actually upsets me more than the lie. I'll tell you this," she asserted. "If my husband and Petey-Parv Pritchet get to go to Dainty Shakes, then you and I are going to the Lady Eyebrow Emporium for a toe knuckle wax."

After the Big Rug Bowling Ball Disaster—the night us boys went to the firepit to listen to the *Friday night shoot 'em up cowboy western story*—we snatched a bottle of Ormish hooch from Mr. Neff's beer box and saw Mrs. Neff outside barefoot. But it was too dark to see exactly how hairy her toe knuckles were.

That night at the firepit, Larry told a great story about being assaulted by Redman earlier that morning.

"We both spotted a mint on the floor at The Manhole and slid out of our booths at the same time, but Redman threw his hat and hit me right in the eye."

Larry leaned his head close to the fire so we could see his bruised eye and continued detailing the morning's events.

"I yelled, 'You wanna dance old man?' Which totally got Redman fired up," Larry laughed as he recalled the incident. "Redman popped the mint in his mouth and went off on a classic Redman rant right there in the middle of the restaurant.

Larry stood up, trying his best to impersonate Redman. "*A shimmy shimmy? A shimmy shimmy from a hoot hoot, like 'a greedy water crane is what ya are. Nope! Not in my day… I tell you, shoots!*

"Redman's behavior was completely inappropriate," Larry said as he plopped down on a stump next to Chad. "Considering everyone was there to talk about saving the Huggabee sisters."

"What happened to the Huggabees?" Ronny inquired.

Larry bit into a smore and mumbled, "Well, rumor has it that the Huggabees got trapped at the top of the Ferris Wheel Chapel when the motor went out last week. They jumped from the Ferris wheel onto a fireman's trampoline and bounced a mile high.

No one's seen them since. If the Huggabees got caught in the Jetstream…they're good as gone!"

Right in the middle of Larry's story, an advertisement came on the radio and said, *"Are you a young ambitious gentleman that loves water? Let your future flow with AquaFlow Water Co."*

The boys and I knew exactly who the voice on the radio was speaking to, The Navy Blue! Chad's eyes lit up as soon as he heard the word water. That was the first time I'd ever thought about any of us boys leaving the town of Big Rug. But right then and there, I knew Chad was good as gone... Just like those poor Huggabee girls.

Six weeks after graduating high school, Chad headed east to a tropical beach town called New Jersey. I hear the sun never sets on the palm trees of New Jersey. But I've never been, so I can only imagine its splendor. I bet the warm sun soaks right into your skin while gazing upon the lush landscape of a place like New Jersey.

Mama used to tell Boof and I, "No one gets wet without making a splash." I guess it was Chad's time to make a splash. I suppose anything that stays in water long enough eventually drifts away, but that doesn't make waving goodbye any easier.

It feels like a lifetime since I last saw Chad's face; but somehow, I see him everywhere I go, and in everything I do. I hold an image of that bald-headed bastard in my mind, forever hoping it might be real. That in the dark, I might reach out; and his hairless head I would feel.

I've heard The Navy Blue is still swimming freestyle off the sunny shores of New Jersey to this very day. And although not the brightest kid, he found a way to land a successful career in the corporate world as a part-time junior auditor of accounts receivable at the AquaFlow Water Bottling Company. A big shot suit 'n tie guy...

I like to imagine that Chad wears his swim trunks under his fancy suit 'n tie while workin' his nine-to-five. That his bald head glistens under the fluorescent lights of his cubicle like the afternoon sun on a stagnant lake.

Truth is, I admire Chad for taking a chance. For diving in head first. For making the bet...the bet on himself. And from what I've been told, he found a way to get wet. Just like the boy I always knew... The Navy Blue.

A man with no feet can never lose his shoes.

— Yoderian proverb

REDMAN'S BAPTISM

My grampy had a saying, "Where you're born, is where they'll mourn." But if that were true, there'd be very few people buried in the Big Rug Cemetery and Pee-Wee Football Field. Because most folks aren't actually born in Big Rug.

The nearest hospital is ninety minutes east of town in Plumpstin City. Big Rug has a private bus that shuttles pregos to the hospital. The Big Rug Birthing Bus—commonly referred to as the B.R. Double-B—was donated by Dr. Gozer. Technically it's a hearse, but it's a big one that sits a few people in the back.

Dr. Gozer was the only full-time family doc when I was a boy. Dr. Plakas, down at Mesozoic Ear-a, was an ENT; so, he wasn't much help for the aches 'n shakes or stomach bubbles. And Brant's mother, Tulip, has always split her clinic hours between the Big Rug Feel Good Building and the Plumpstin City Hospital; so she's tough to track down in an emergency.

The *Big Rug Repository* wrote an article about the B.R. Double-B the year Dr. Gozer retired. When asked about his investment in the shuttle service, Dr. Gozer was quoted as saying, "Birth is a magical thing, but no one wants to see that. Let them city folks over in Plumpstin City clean up that mess."

Plumpstin City was named after the first Red Maple Rodeo Miss Teen Bonnet beauty pageant winner, Flumper Plumpstin. A young farm girl from Chigger Bottom.

Flumper went by her middle name, Robert. Even when shortened to *Flump* or *Ump,* the name Flumper doesn't exactly elicit the image of a beautiful young woman. So, Flumper went by Robert, which she shortened to Bert; for a touch of femininity. And I'm here to tell you, Bert was definitely feminine. There might not be photos of Bert's beauty, but I've seen paintings.

The first time I saw an image of Bert was when our third-grade class took a field trip to the Big Rug Magazine Library and Coupon Trading Post. Pucker Loaf painted a portrait of Bert, and man...that guy knows what he's doing with a paint brush. He got all the details right! Bert was a Bettie... No doubt! That gal's skin was golden as a corndog's crust! She was the sexiest woman I'd seen since Lunch Lady Irwin wore a low-cut blouse to school.

Although most Big Rugians aren't born in Big Rug, we still mourn in Big Rug. Because where you're born isn't nearly as important as where you've lived. And round these parts, folks take pride in the place they live. So, when Larry's family moved to town from somewhere south of the Dustfog Region, it got a lot of people's attention. And not just because they were black...

Shortly after moving to Big Rug, Larry rode his saddle-dog out to Redman's farm for a little coon-cat chasin' and ended up getting the whole town into a tizzy.

Folks weren't sure what to think about the new family in town, but Larry wasn't shy about making an introduction. And he made one hell of an introduction! The boys and I refer to that day's events as Redman's Baptism... But at the time, Sheriff Beitzel just called it simple assault.

According to the police report, Redman was stacking cinderblocks around the base of his corn silo when he felt a rain drop tickle the back of his neck. He looked up, but there wasn't a cloud in the sky. He went back to his task and felt another sprinkle on his neck. He looked up again to a sky clear 'n blue; yet raindrops continued to fall upon his head.

"It's a divine miracle," Redman declared. "Rain from the sea!"

The old man fell to his knees with tears in his eyes as the rain gently fell upon his face. He lifted his head and opened his arms wide to the heavens, believing he was about to be lifted into God's great kingdom.

"Oh Lord Father, forgive these old hands that've held too many drinks. Forgive this mouth that has cursed and gossiped," Redman pleaded, licking the raindrops off his lips.

"Lord, let this salty rain baptize me into a new man, oh Lord Father! This water from the sea that's falling on me... Holy water! Moses water," he sobbed and shook his hands at the sky. *"Part da seas, Moses! Part da seas!"*

It wasn't until Redman opened his eyes that he saw the heavenly rain drops from the sea weren't falling from the sky. The holy salt water of the Lord was streaming from Larry's little ding-dong from atop the corn silo.

Larry had no idea he was pissing on Redman, nor was he aware of the spiritual awakening taking place on the ground. Larry simply saw something tall and thought, "I'd like to climb that!"

So, what's a boy to do when he finds himself at the top of a fifty-foot tower? Take a waz off the edge of course! And that's exactly what Larry did! His tiny-tike tinkler waterfalled right off the edge of that corn silo...and right onto Redman's head!

And that's when Shiffy and the sheriff were called onto the scene, triggering a crowd of folks to congregate around Redman's corn silo to see the new kid in town stuck on top.

"I'm staying," Larry announced down to Sheriff Beitzel. "There's a pillow and a blanket up here... And a half-eaten sandwich. And a bottle of wine, I think? I'm not sure... It tastes terrible though."

"Hey... That's mine!" Preacher Jepp shouted. "Oops," he gulped, realizing his error.

"That's mine...ers... I mean, that's why *minors* shouldn't drink," he looked around at the crowd, doing his best to play it cool while avoiding the angry scowl of several young ladies.

"Son," Sheriff Beitzel hollered. "I ain't gettin' dirty this early in the week! Town don't pay for this uniform...or the cleaning."

Which explained the safety pins holding the Sheriff's shirt together where his fat belly popped a button.

"Get on down from there son," he demanded. "I'm due for second dinner in thirty!"

Shiffy adjusted his deputy hat and sighed, "Ain't dat da trute."

"Shut it, Shiffy!" the sheriff chided. "I needs the protein. I'm building bulk. Fat to mass Shiffy! Fat to mass... That's how it works! Heard Dr. Plakas say it."

Redman walked up growling and waving his handkerchief in the air, "You there... Ugly man!"

"Me?" Muhck mumbled, looking around confused.

"Yes, you," Redman fumed. "Get that dang boy off 'a that dang silo. You a critter expert ain't ya?"

Muhck wiped his nose on his wrist and sauntered forward, pulling his cutoff army shorts up over his love handles.

"See na see, this a boy-critter. Boy-critter a tough critter... Ever try gettin' a tree kid out a tree?" Muhck asked as we struggled to understand what the heck he was saying. "It's tough. Boy-critter a tough critter, see na see!"

I looked over at my Uncle Shty, who was scratching his head as if trying to jump-start the engine of his brain.

"You got that coyot outta Cornbread's shed last fall," Uncle Shty reminded Muhck. "I mean, coyots are smart! They have to be smart as a kid."

"Cornbread cornbread!" Cornbread advised Muhck. "Cornbread cornbread...cornbread."

"See na see, now we's gettin' somewhere," Muhck declared. "Works for a coyot, gotsta work for a boy-critter I reckon?"

Muhck reached into his backpack, pulled out some bird seed mixed with raisins, and sprinkled it around the edge of the silo.

"See na see, now we's wait for the critter boy to catch the scent. Critters can't resist my critter mix. Me 'n Mimi make all our critter mix by hand," Muhck bragged while randomly taking off his shirt.

"Do you have any with beef jerky?" Gus politely inquired.

"See na see, that's the exotic mixes," Muhck excitedly chimed. "What type 'a exotic critter you after? Probably a brush-rooster or a flat back bobbycat if you needin' a meat blend."

"Why gosh-darn it," Redman vented and threw his old baseball cap at Muhck. "These dang trouble trousers... Rock pigeons I say... Gimmie gimmie too-toos, flippin' in the too-toos... No sir... Bustin' up the place like a...like a...mischief-makin' weaver finch."

Redman stomped back to his farmhouse, mumbling along the way, "Skippy dippy ding-a-lings to all of yas... *Nope!* Not in my day...I tell you, shoots!"

While everyone was watching Redman explode into one of his classic rants, Larry tossed the BLT sandwich he found at the top of the corn silo over the edge and hit Sheriff Beitzel in the head. That's when the fireworks started...literally!

Every Big Rugian man carries firecrackers in his pockets in case of an emergency. Pops only wore cargo shorts in the summer, so he'd have plenty of room for bottle rockets.

"This'll get 'em down," Sheriff Beitzel smirked while lighting a roman candle.

Uncle Shty tossed an M-80 into the air and hollered, "Pocket-cracker time!"

"See na see, this a last resort when gettin' a critter..." Muhck snorted while rummaging through his backpack. "But it's effective. Burned down a shed with powder poppers once. But got that critter out... Black kat crackin'... Booyah!"

At that point, everyone started lightin' up. The powder poppers were exploding all around us. It was chaos! But folks seemed to be enjoying themselves. Until Sheriff Beitzel took a bottle rocket to the ass, that is.

"I'm hit," the fat man squealed, throwing his baton in the air at the fireworks. "Third time this week damn it. Shoot them fireworks, Shiffy. Probable cause!"

Shiffy quickly bent his knees, stuck out his tongue, closed one eye to take aim, and shot his revolver in the air at a bottle rocket. The gunshot blast startled every dang animal within a hundred yards. Muff-cows, round-horned oboes, cotton-haired mules, you name it; they all popped up running.

"Dear Lord," the sheriff yelped, zig-zagging and trying to avoid the stampeding animals and exploding fireworks. "Damn it, Shiffy... Save me!"

I've never seen a fat man make lateral movements as quickly as Sheriff Beitzel did that day. He looked like a chubby matador dodging a bull's horns. Until he slipped on a Duck Dog duck-log and landed hard on his back.

"Oh hell... My sister and I share these shoes," he moaned, lying on his back, trying to elevate his dog dirt soiled foot off the ground.

As we watched the chaos unfold, other folks around town started shooting off fireworks too. There were pocket-poppers going off everywhere. We were less than a month out from the Fourth of July, so folks around town were stocked with all kinds of personal explosives.

My grampy used to say, "Nine times outta ten, if you see someone doing something, you should do it too... Nine times outta ten it'll work in your favor... It's math!"

It seemed like the whole town was shooting off fireworks on the day of Redman's Baptism. While folks were laughing and enjoying the show, Larry climbed down without anyone really noticing. But that'd be the last time Larry went unnoticed in the town of Big Rug.

How he climbed up that corn silo at such a young age, I'll never know. The kid was a physical freak from the time he was born. An athlete like none of us had ever seen before. The type of athlete that gets admiration from supporters and condemnation from rivals. And it didn't take long before Larry had his fair share of rivals.

Mumper may be a little pumpkin town, but once a year, it holds the biggest event in the Dustfog Region, Fall Fest! The annual event brings in folks from every nook 'n cranny of the region to eat, drink, play games, and buy pumpkins for their fall decorations.

But, as great as the pumpkin attractions are at Fall Fest, the main event is the Lumberers of the Valley tournament. Oh... My... Lumber... Jack... It's exciting! Once a year, the top lumberjacks from across the Dustfog Region descend on the little town of Mumper to compete in the greatest lumberjack competition known to man.

Lumberers of the Valley is such an important event to Big Rugians, that it's part of our school curriculum. And Larry couldn't get enough of the history behind the tournament.

Some folks study the Greek Gods, but Larry's wisdom came from the lumberers who notched their spot into the history books of the tournament. And his all-time favorite historical figure is a guy named The Ormish Oak!

Larry always dressed up as The Ormish Oak for Halloween. And he'd start wearing his costume months in advance.

"I'm breaking it in," he'd say.

"It's July," one of us boys would remind him.

It became an annual tradition that while trick-or-treating, Larry would tell us the story of "The Tumble of the Lumber that Killed The Ormish Oak."

The history books say the Lumberers of the Valley tournament started as a method for claiming lumber lands. Instead of fighting over resources, towns competed in acts of skill. And in the early days, there was a goliath of a man they called The Ormish Oak, who was the best lumberjack to ever swing an axe.

Many believe the man was carved from a giant oak tree struck by lightning in one of God's Great Storms on Mrs. Yoder's Mountain. Others say he grew to the size of three men with the help of some kinda ancient Asian wizardry. But Larry told us when the Ormish Oak's mother was pregnant, she ate the beating heart of a crown-horned bison, and that's how he grew to be a giant.

Beer Man Neff said the Ormish Oak's nostrils were the size of porridge bowls, and his hands were wide as a bull's ass. I'll remind you that Mr. Neff was our high school history teacher, a position they don't just give to anyone. Folks have to fill out an application without misspelling a single word to be a high school teacher in Big Rug. So, Mr. Neff knew what he was talkin' 'bout!

The Ormish Oaks axe is displayed on the History Wall at the Big Rug Magazine Library and Coupon Trading Post. The axe's handle is a rounded six-by-six post of solid Yoderian Cliff Oak; the only wood strong enough to support the weight of its twenty-five-pound steel head.

To this day, no person has held the Ormish Oak's axe off the ground for longer than five seconds; a record held by the Mountain Mouse of Mumper…Millie Grontrouder!

The Mountain Mouse of Mumper dominated the Lumberers of the Valley tournament back when my folks were younger. She's also my father's favorite "golden-era" lumberjack.

And the reason why Mama "always" had to wear a black wig, with nautical rope-sized pigtails, as her Halloween costume when I was a kid. Pops insisted…

A few years before the Bad Juice Decade, back when my grandparents were kids, the Ormish Oak was out workin' the wood deep in the forest of Owdina National Park. He was cuttin' 'n stackin' like a lumberjack jackin'. But he was cuttin' too big and stackin' too high, resulting in a twenty-foot pile of lumber to break loose from a snapped strap and bury the Ormish Oak alive.

The tree trunks were so big, and he was so deep in the forest, that no one could possibly save him. To this day, we still don't have the technology to know how a single man was able to stack tree trunks twenty feet high.

Mr. Neff had us read an old *Plumpstin City Chronicles* newspaper article about The Ormish Oak while studying the local history of the Dustfog Region. The article was written by the editor-in-chief of the paper and recounts the day he saw The Ormish Oak with his own eyes. The article reads:

> *"Today, whilst walking Dust Fog Market, I stood in the shadow of a man with shoulders wide as a temper-crank. I mistakenly, and painfully, bumped my head against his forearm. A forearm dense as a chiseled block of granite.*
>
> *"The local lumberjacks refer to him as The Ormish Oak; a name fitting for a man whose finger nails were thick as a leather belt. His neck was so big that his Adam's apple beard had the girth of a lard sac.*

"By my estimates, the Ormish Oak easily stood eight feet tall with a weight just north of a female barn-hog. Like many of you, the Ormish culture, and its people, are of a great mystery to me. But I believe the large man to be just that... A man.

"Not a hairless sasquatch birthed by Mrs. Yoder's Mountain. Not an extraterrestrial life form sent to Earth to consume our women and children for galactical population control. And he is certainly not a mythical creature created by ancient Oriental wizards to flatten our mountains; as I once suggested in this very newspaper.

"I tell you this, my fellow settlers, do not fear The Ormish Oak. Although terrifying in stature, I saw a kindness in his Ormish eyes.

"He spoke to me with a baritone so deep, it raddled my rib cage. I claim not to be a translator of Yoderian Dutch, but I believe The Ormish Oak looked down at me and said,

'Erka burka ye purkle shtick owder ear?'
Translation; 'Do they have pickle sticks over there?'

"And so, I ask you, the fine townsmen of the Dustfog Region; what kind of monster enjoys the same delicacies as you or I? No monster at all I say...
No monster at all."

Shortly after Redman's Baptism, the boys and I officially invited Larry to join our friend group. How could anyone not want to be friends with the kid that wazzed on Redman's head?

All of us enjoyed introducing Larry to the intricacies of the place he now called home, but there was nothing like the time we took him to watch his first Lumberers of the Valley tournament.

Larry's first tournament experience was truly a historic moment. It was the first time in the modern era that a Big Rugian lumberjack placed first in the tournament. A guy who worked for the city as a porta potty flusher took the grand prize. He was part of a group of city workers who train and compete in the tournament every year.

They call themselves, "Meckler's Mud Loggers." The name pays homage to the historical political activist, Meckler the Heckler, who "heckled" Big Rug officials—while they used the restroom—until they funded public porta potties to be placed around town.

Meckler the Heckler is a personal inspiration of mine and a hero in the civil rights movement of Big Rug. Simply put, Meckler was a figure of elegance in a time of humiliation. He was a voice of anguish, an image of possibility, and a prophet in the crusade for an accommodating society for those who choose to exercise their right to bowel release on demand; as any decent physician would recommend a person do! Holding things in will mess you up! Aunt Sara says her receding hairline is from holding in her number twos!

"No bowel control, won't wait till I'm old. When I gotsta go, I gotsta go," Meckler chanted as he heckled folks in the restroom of city hall.

I got pretty deep into his legacy movement in my early thirties. Some people are just called to be part of something bigger than themselves. I was a "Meckler Heckler" to the bone. No doubt!

I'm proud to say I was part of the "Down with the Wheel" movement back in my hecklin' days. Everywhere you looked back then, there were wheels: on cars, on bikes, on roller skates, on watches, on blenders, and all kinds of other stuff... Quite frankly, the wheel issue still persists today. All the while, the corporate fat cats of the big wheel industry enrich themselves by pushing wheels on the common man; and contributing to the engineerical systemic injustice of our communities.

One day, us Meckler Hecklers decided to take the fight right to the wheel. So we heckled down at the old folk's home; demanding a ban on wheels being unethically attached to chairs.

"*Squares are in! Monopolies are out! Down with the wheel! I scream, I shout!*" we protested while waving our picket signs.

The idea of the big wheel industry taking advantage of those dumb old bastards still gets me hot. Them geriatric wrinkle-bags deserve better. My fellow Meckler Hecklers, and I, protested at the entrance of the old folk's home for two weeks straight, forcing management to implement a three-month ban on wheelchairs... Fight the power!

"*It's Not the Chair, It's the Wheels,*" was the front-page headline in the *Big Rug Repository*. The nursing home had saddle-dogs drag the elderly around on sleds during the three-month ban. *And...*I might add...hip replacements went up by forty percent. *Proving*—in my opinion—that the big wheel industry wanted the elderly to have bad bones! Otherwise, they would've replaced their hips before they ever broke... And for free!

But, I'm no hero... Just a regular guy doing hero stuff!

Kingdoms are not built by kings;
for the body of a bat,
is just a rat if not for wings.

— Ormish scripture

DEAD TREE CEMETERY

Owdina National Park is an upside-down U-shaped mountain range with Lake Stoolmist nestled in the middle. The open top of the U—the south—is the separating border between Big Rug and Stoolmist. As much as I despise the town of Stoolmist, even I can admit that the lake is breathtaking. And I'm not just saying that because of my asthma, which tends to flare up in higher elevations.

Grampy and Pops surprised me with a sunrise fishing trip on Lake Stoolmist for my tenth birthday. We rowed Grampy's old wooden canoe out to the middle of the lake and just sat there…soaking in the beauty of our surroundings.

On our way out, I saw Pucker Loaf painting one of his "nudes" on a dock. The man was just standing out there on the edge of that dock, buck-ass-naked, paintin' a paintin'.

One of Pucker Loaf's nude paintings is about the price of a modified mud-spud; so, I've never seen one in person. But I see Pucker paintin' his nudes at least once a quarter. The man paints naked all-around town….

You're grocery shoppin' at Thrifty Foods; there's buck-naked Pucker by the bruised berries bin, paintin' a nude. Enjoying an evening meal at Meat-a-Tatoes; there's Pucker, showin' sausage while paintin' sausage. Doin' some shoppin' at Stuff & Stuff's Nice Things; there's Pucker, naked in the nick-nack aisle.

Heck, the day Ronny took the Love Walk and proposed to Barb at her high school graduation, Pucker was backstage—naked as a skinned potato—paintin' a nude. It was a little weird… I'll admit that. But, the man's an artistic genius… It would be unbecoming to question the methods of a man with his brilliance? And I'm not about to become unbecoming.

I've never felt smaller than when I was sitting on Lake Stoolmist, surrounded by the high forests of Owdina National Park, with Mrs. Yoder's Mountain towering above us to the north. Even the velvety white clouds looked bigger as they moseyed on by, occasionally blocking the sun from shooting its shimmering rays of light deep into the water's depth.

It was a great day until some Stoolmist yuppie-guppy told us we were trespassing on a private lake. Stoolmist may be beautiful, but the people have a way of making things ugly.

I'll tell you this about the people of Stoolmist, they don't share bars of soap with each other… Nope! I swear on Grampy and Granny's grave they don't. Each family has "their own" bar of soap… I don't care how nice the community is, if a neighbor ain't sharin' soap with a neighbor…I ain't interested in bein' a neighbor.

Them Junkmist richie riches love to brag about their fancy sidewalks and single-use toilet paper. And how they use mulch in their flower beds instead of white rock. Mulch…that stuff lasts a year at best… Rocks—or if you can afford it, fish tank gravel—lasts forever. A fish tank gravel flower bed is a thing of beauty. And the gravel comes in different colors, so you can really get your "flower beds 'a buzzin','" as the feather foots say.

Pinky-pointers know a thing or two about flowerbed design. Aunt Sara hired a limp wrist to do her landscaping. He wore a lady's scarf and would kiss the flowers after planting them. Odd guy…but brilliant with fish tank gravel. He made one side of the flowerbed light purple and the other side neon orange. Talk about stylish!

Grampy, Pops, and I rowed the canoe into shore after being harassed by that yuppie-guppy stool-bag and headed home for an early lunch. While driving through the winding dirt roads of Owdina National Park, I briefly saw three young women, in thick wool dresses, walking down a path with baskets of eggs.

"There go some 'a them Ishmaelians," Grampy nudged Pops.

"What's an Ishmaelian?" I inquired from the back.

"The Ishmaelians live in Bewster Grove," Pops told me. "Bewster Grove is a tiny chicken farm community that sits on the edge of Big Rug and Owdina National Park. Folks around town call it a "cult community.""

"The Bewster family has been squatting on a small piece of land since before you were born. They call themselves The People's Awakening of Ishmaelians. Strange bunch if you ask me."

Shortly after the Bewster family started squatting on the land, one of the fellas put a sign up that read Bewster Grove. Technically, Bewster Grove wasn't recognized within the Dustfog Region, and technically, they didn't have any rights to the land. But the sign looked so good that Mayor Deradodo decided to just leave them alone. And they had the least expensive eggs around.

"Two dozen eggs for a dime," Mayor Deradodo said while discussing Bewster Grove. "Ain't gonna be the one to screw that up. Sweet deals like that are a rarity! Don't give a damn if they squattin'.

If they farmin' chicken, they makin' a livin'. So, let's just consider the land to be givin'."

Behind Bewster Grove is an area called Dead Tree Cemetery. All the trees died from cankers around the time of the Bad Juice Decade. But right in the middle of Dead Tree Cemetery, alive and well, stands a colossal cypress tree. It's the tallest tree on record in the Dustfog Region. If you have the guts to climb to the top of the old cypress, it's called climbing to The Top of the World.

There are stories about kids trying to climb the tree and falling to their death. Granny knew a boy that climbed up the tree and couldn't climb down. He was so high up that no one could save him. A tree kid that never climbed down… Rumor has it his skeleton is still up there today.

It was at the Honey Farm Fair in the last week of May when Preston, the golden-haired leader of the Ferry Flowers, challenged Larry to The Top of the World. A boy doesn't forget a day like that, for fear has an enduring effect on one's memory.

That year, the boys and I had our eyes peeled for a new food stand making its debut at the Honey Farm Fair.

"I'm telling you," Gus stressed while leading us boys around the fair on a wild goose chase, "last month, I went to Plumpstin City with my sister… *She's in college, okay*," he added braggadociously, zigzagging through the crowd. "Her buddy Ray-Ray and I are really close… Y'all wouldn't get it…because you're just kids."

"First," Dale interrupted, "you're like the third youngest of all of us Gus. Second," he snatched a jerky stick from Gus's back pocket. "What I'm hearing you say, *basically*…is that your sister—*and her boyfriend*—took you to Plumpstin City."

"Can I just tell the story Dale?" Gus sighed. "Ray-Ray and I…not my sister…ate at a place called Plumpstin City Shaved Ice Condiments. It's incredible! We had every flavor except ballpark mustard. They mix relish in with the ice! Relish you guys! My mom said they're here somewhere, so just keep looking!"

When we found the Plumpstin City Shaved Ice Condiments stand, there was a line wrapping all the way to the Turkey-Tongue-On-A-Stick booth. Which didn't bother us because Bozo Goober was slappin' the spoons right next to the booth. Man…that guy can play a mean set 'a spoons!

Back in the day, Bozo Goober and the Spoons in the Spotlight toured every town in the Dustfog Region. "Gotta play to get paid," Bozo would say.

Nowadays, Bozo only performs in the parking lots of dirt track stockcar races in exchange for free admission and a foot-long hotdog. Bozo Goober… A man livin' the dream!

Everyone at the fair was dancin' to Bozo's jammin'.

"*Whew…*" Marie-Agnus sang out from across the winding line. "Spank them spoons Bozo," she cheered while spinning in the ecstasy of Bozo's cover song, "It's a Grand Old Flag."

The Zapinsky sisters grabbed Marie-Agnus's hand and moved their bodies like an hourglass made of Jello. Those girls had curves like a roll'e coast'e… And I was on for the ride. No doubt!

While all of us were groovin' to Bozo's soulful spoonin', I noticed the Ferry Flowers of Stoolmist and the Three Blind Bats standing in line with us. And—I might add—they were the only buzz-kills not dancing. The Goob was slappin' the spoons like a def-man crankin' the tunes; and those jerkwads weren't even nodding their heads.

It was just two months ago that those sally sacks TP'd the sign at Don't Drink Paint Supply and burnt "Ass Weasels" in the grass. The boys and I approached them with an intensity that radiated across all of the innocent fairgoers standing in line with us.

"Well, well, well. Look Sofia, it's the Boys of Big *Slug*," Preston mocked while looking around for laughs like a butt-weed. "I'm surprised you porridge brains are even allowed out in society after the stunt you pulled at our indoor pool. That's a publicly funded facility you scabs damaged!" he chastised us like a wannabe man of the law.

Mitch stepped forward from behind us, popped the collar on his black leather jacket and countered, "That publicly funded facility you call a pool looks like a shaved muff-cow with chickenpox. It's a piece of junk compared to the Don't Drink Paint Supply sign. That sign was hand painted by Pucker Loaf damn it! The man's a regional treasure!"

"Oooh...look gents." Preston teased and turned toward his friends. "*It's me, Mitch.* I wear a leather jacket in the summer... And my fly's down!"

The Three Blind Bats started snickering in the background.

"Where's your Fly-Down friends Mitch?" Bucktooth Hudson laughed with his stupid overbite. "Kissing a cat somewhere?"

Hudson was a bucktoothed grass stain. I'm sure he still is today. The kid used to tuck his winter jacket into his khakis. Who does that? And, who wears khakis in the winter? Get some jeans you jerk!"

"You lumberjack like ladies," Chad yelled.

"Yawp," Brant added with perfect timing.

"No," Stinkin' Lincoln screamed. "*You* lumberjack like ladies."

"I've always been a fan of ladies..." Gus spoke softly with a smile and winked at Isabella.

The tension was thicker than a Duck Dog duck-log. Both sides were ready to pounce the other. Mitch and Preston locked eyes like two boxers before a fight. The sweet rhythms of Bozo Goober slappin' the spoons to an aggressive rendition of "This Land Is Your Land" electrified the air around us.

"You Ferry Flowers couldn't crank a pitch 'n whittle if your elbows were greased in corn oil," Mitch mocked as the Three Blind Bats covered their mouths in shock. They'd clearly never heard an insult that awesome before.

"You don't know jack squat," Fat Neck Oliver screamed from somewhere in the back.

Preston stepped toward Mitch while aggressively taking off his Stoolmist ballcap.

"Shut your dirty mouth, Mitch. Or I'll shut it for you!" he threatened through clenched teeth.

A stare down ensued between us boys and the Ferry Flowers that must've lasted thirty seconds... No blinking... The first sign of weakness is always the first to blink. Lazy eyes included. No exceptions.

"Excuse me, are you boys in line?" asked an unsuspecting mother enjoying the fair with her children.

Neither side dared respond to her...for fear of risking an inadvertent blink or twitch. In my peripheral, I could see her kids watching us with ice-cream cones and balloons in hand. I'm sure in awe of the stare down unfolding in front of them.

"Are you boys in line for the shaved ice condiments," she politely leaned in, trying to elicit an answer.

The stare down felt like I was riding a firework shooting into the sky, knowing at any moment there'd be an explosion. With each silent second, the two sides became more enraged.

"I'm going to move ahead in line if you boys are just messing around," the mother lectured while pulling her children past us.

I could feel my eyes drying as I struggled not to blink. But then, out of nowhere, a trash cat jumped on Mitch's shoulder at the exact moment Bozo Goober started slappin' the spoons to "Yankee Doodle." The cat casually licked some dried maple syrup Mitch had spilled on the collar of his jacket a few days earlier. It was the coolest thing us boys had ever seen! All those Stoolmist jerks stepped back in shock. Mitch looked badass with that cat perched on his shoulder! Like a superhero or something.

In an attempt to regain control of the situation, Preston aggressively turned away from Mitch and shoved Larry's shoulder.

"I challenge you to The Top of the World," Preston called out for all to hear, opening his arms wide and spinning slowly in a circle.

There was an unspoken rivalry that'd been building for years between Larry and Preston. Us boys knew Preston was jealous of Larry's athleticism. Folks were always debating on who was the better athlete. It was only a matter of time before the two collided head-to-head and put an end to the debate once and for all.

But this was no athletic event. This was no game. And it definitely wasn't the old corn silo out at Redman's farm. This was The Top of the World! And none of us were prepared for something like that!

"Don't do it Larry," Ronny whispered while maintaining an aggressive scowl at Stinkin' Lincoln. "It's not worth it. Last week, I tripped and hit my shoulder on a tree and got a splinter from the bark... Tree bark splinters are the worst Larry!"

"What's wrong?" Oliver grinned. "Are ya yella?"

"I bet your undies are yellow too," Hudson added like a dork. "Cause you peed in them... Cause you're a chicken... *Bark, bark... Bark, bark!*"

"That's a dog you buck-toothed dipstick," Mitch squabbled. "*Bawk, bawk* is a chicken, dummy!"

Preston poked Larry in the chest and growled, "You might be a big shot in *Big Suck*, but in Stoolmist, you're just another benchwarmer."

Larry stepped closer to Preston while rolling his shoulders back and cracking his neck to the side like a total stud muffin and replied, "I accept!"

"It's on," Preston fumed with fire in his eyes.

"To the Top of the World," Hudson screeched like a girl.

"Yawp," Brant bellowed, throwing his half-eaten chicken parm pita at Hudson and splattering red sauce all over his shirt.

Next thing I knew, we were running through the Honey Farm Fair toward the exit.

"I didn't get a ballpark mustard shaved ice yet guys..." Gus whined. "Fellas, wait. Don't go... They mix relish in with the ice! Relish fellas... *Relish*!"

We left the fair with a kind of excitement only found in youthful ignorance. The cool breeze sent goosebumps across my body, like tits tingling when the milk comes in. We piled into our cars and sped out of the fair and into the night.

The twenty-minute drive north felt like seconds as a feverishness of delirium suspended our consciousness. We laughed in the dirt road's dust as the big tree appeared over the foothills.

"There it is," Ronny trepidatiously pointed.

The giant cypress stood stoic, high above the tree line, like a tower of doom gleaming in the moonlight. Heat lightning flickered through the clouds as thunder gently rumbled in the distance.

To this day, I've never felt the heebie-jeebies like I did when we pulled up to Dead Tree Cemetery in the stillness of night. That place was creepier than a shaved hen-horse. It looked like the brittle trees were drowning in fog. The moonbeams illuminated the misty air, capturing the crisscrossing shadows of the crippled trees as if holding their silhouettes in a prison of haze.

"This place is weird… Let's go back to the fair," Haley suggested as owls hooted around us.

"I agree," Andrea trembled, clutching her sister's arm. "I have a bad feeling about this place."

"You want to back out too Larry?" Preston spouted arrogantly.

Stinkin' Lincoln laughed while pulling Ava under his arm. "Yeah, Big Rug boys can't even climb stairs, let alone a tree. Isn't that right Clumsy Klutz?"

"It's *Captain* Klutz!" Chad quickly defended Ronny.

"Did someone fart?" Ronny pretended to sniff the air. "Or is Stincoln breathing with his mouth open?"

"Yawp," Brant added as a few of the girls giggled with us at Lincoln's expense.

Lincoln, red with embarrassment, shouted, "You're the fart mouth…or…fart breath person…or…just…whatever! Just shut up, you Deradodo dork!"

Ronny and Lincoln continued to trade insults as we walked through the fog with our arms lifted above our waist like we were wading through a shallow pond.

"The fog is so thick I can't see my house slippers," Dale quivered as we arrived at the base of the towering cypress.

"Last chance Larry," Preston taunted, walking up to the tree and smacking it with a few deep thuds.

"Stop being dare devils," Marie-Agnus begged. "Haven't you heard the stories about this place? People die here. A few years back, the Huggabee sisters were flying kites at Bewster Grove while their parents shopped for eggs. Their kites got tangled in this tree. They climbed up and got stuck! The firemen's ladders couldn't reach them, and the Huggabees starved to death. Their bodies are still up there," she cried out.

"No, no, no," Gus chimed, stepping in and waving his hands. "The Huggabees didn't starve… That was a different kid a long time ago. Tuck's grandma grew up with the kid who starved. The Huggabees were eaten by vultures. The only thing left…" he whispered, slowly looking around for a dramatic effect, "is Andrea Huggabee's back brace!"

An eerie silence ensued as we cautiously scanned our strange surroundings. Out there in the darkness I was nervous as a long-tailed cat sittin' in a room full of rockin' chairs. And then, a bone-chilling scream erupted out from the fog!

"We are the Huggabees," Haley and Andrea shrieked in unison, scaring the bejesus out of us.

"Our mother remarried! You were at the wedding Marie-Agnus," Haley cried as the two sisters stormed away.

"What is wrong with you people…?" Andrea scorned.

Marie-Agnus and Suzie LaCuzzi followed the sisters back to the cars, trying their best to apologize.

"Didn't you girls used to have longer hair or something?" Suzie asked sympathetically.

"They don't look like the Huggabees," Dale grinned, lifting his hands up to his chest in a cupping motion and laughing. "If…you…know…what I mean…? You see what I'm doing…? My hands…? They're boobs!"

"So…?" Hudson scoffed with his stupid buck-teeth.

"They're boobs Hudson," Dale insisted. "Because girls have boobs! It's hilarious… Do you even see my hands right now?"

"What girls have boobs?" Fat Neck Oliver blurted.

"The Huggabees, you donkey tail… Or the Zapinskys, or whatever Haley and Andrea are calling themselves these days. They have boobs… It's not even funny now, so just forget it," Dale sighed in frustration.

"Wait!" Sofia paused and looked around the foggy forest. "Where *are* the Huggabees? They were in Ava's car, right? I swear they were in the car with us."

"Holy cannoli," Hudson said in a panic, frantically fanning at the fog to try and see the ground. "Haley and Andrea probably suffocated in the fog. Some people have weak lungs like that."

"Didn't they just walk back to the cars, like two-minutes ago?" Stinkin' Lincoln asked confused.

"Stincoln," Gus snapped. "Now is not the time to play twenty questions. Grow up, turd tongue."

Isabella's eyes welled with tears. "Those girls seemed so sweet."

"They're dead now," Gus whispered and comforted Isabella. "Hudson is right. Some people have weak lungs… The Huggabees suffocated in the fog. It's time we all come to grips with that if we want to make it outta here alive! Stick with me Isabella," he pulled her in close. "I'll protect you from the fog."

"I've had enough," Preston barked. "Are we climbing or what?"

"I'm ready when you are," Larry said, bumping into Preston with his shoulder as he walked to the tree's giant base.

"Okay, okay." Gus released Isabella from under his arm and pushed his way to the front of the group. "On my count. First to the top wins. If you die…automatic disqualification!"

"Don't do it Preston," Ava whimpered. "Those sweet Huggabee girls are dead. They suffocated in the fog Preston… In the fog," she dramatically collapsed into Sofia's arms.

"Our mother remarried," a faint cry echoed in the distance from our parked cars.

"When I say beef cigar," Gus instructed, shifting our attention back to him.

He pulled a jerky stick out of his back pocket and tossed it in his mouth like some sort of pre-game ritual.

"Ready…"

He stepped back from the tree, rolling his jerky stick from one side of his mouth to the other.

"Set…"

He slightly bent his knees and opened his arms wide.

"Run!" Oliver jumped in front of Gus, squealing with the full force of his fat neck as flashlights beamed through the fog.

"It's the Ishmaelians," Ava cried. "I can't wear cult clothing. Wool is not my fabric," she shrieked as the Three Blind Bats scattered into the forest.

"Isabela, wait," Gus implored, reaching his open hand out into the fog. "You'll suffocate like the Huggabees."

"All right, ya dang whiskey whiskers," Sheriff Beitzel grunted as he stumbled down an embankment, huffin' and puffin' with each step. "What y'all doin' out here? Where ya at?"

"It's Shiffy and Shitzel," Preston announced while running through the trees.

"We didn't kill the Huggabees," Hudson pleaded from a distance. "They suffocated in the fog!"

The sheriff stumbled up to us while biting into a chocolate bar. His cheeks were flush from the brisk walk in the forest as he tugged his loose trousers over his belly.

"Them Bewsters say y'all makin' a ruckus," he griped while trying to catch his breath. "Say it soundin' like an ex-wife meetin' a new wife."

"Ain't dat da trute," Shiffy yelped, popping outta the fog and terrifying all of us.

As the sheriff flailed his arms in fright, he accidently dropped his chocolate bar.

"Ding dang doggone it, Shiffy. That's the last chocolate," he berated and smacked Shiffy with his hat. "You know I gots the low blood sugars."

He picked up the chocolate bar from off the ground and gently dusted off the debris with his fingertips.

"Wrapper protected it. Still good. Tragedy obverted," the sheriff said biting into the chocolate.

The lawmen scolded us for a while before eventually leaving for last call at the Honey Farm Fair. As their tail lights disappeared into the fog, we noticed the Ferry Flowers and the Three Blind Bats were nowhere to be found. They ran away like a bunch of field mice running from a fox as soon as things got interesting.

But...to be honest, I was secretly relieved we got busted... That was the first, and last time, I made my way to Dead Tree Cemetery. That place was creepy! Who knows what's lurking out there in the darkness, hidden in the fog. Other than the dead bodies of the Huggabees that is...

Larry had a million-dollar idea a few months after The Top of the World nightmare. One evening out at the fire pit, while listening to a *Friday night shoot 'em up cowboy western story,* he asked us boys, "Why go through the trouble of finding a restroom when you could enjoy the convenience, and privacy, of your own pants?" A legitimate question, worthy of a legitimate answer…

The next day, he cut a few trash bags into the shape of underwear—hot glued a bag of cotton balls to the inside—and just like that, Larry created the prototype for Big Ups, *"Now you can go, and no one will know."*

Before the age of eighteen, Larry had created one of the first versions of what we now call adult diapers, and the town of Big Rug couldn't get enough! Big Rugians tend to gravitate toward a fried food diet. Which is, in part, the reason the average person in town pops-a-squat roughly six times a day. That's equivalent to an hour a day spent on the toilet. Larry found a way for Big Rugians to get that hour and a half back!

It started with the football team. We wore Big Ups to play through practice and games; eliminating the need to take our equipment off to relieve ourselves. Then, the Jazzarate dojo caught on. With Big Ups, folks could stay focused on performing martial arts to the frothy sound of jazz music; even when nature called.

Word really started spreading about the incredible undies when Big Ups were endorsed by the Big Rug Mechanics and Construction Guild. And then Ronny's father used his mayor power to have all city workers wear Big Ups, so they could spend more time on the job and less time on the toilet. Once folks saw a pair of Big Ups peeking out the back of a workin' man's trousers, everyone in town wanted a pair.

"Time is money, ya hear," Mayor Deradodo spoke to a crowd. "Can't flush money down the toilet. Gotta work folks! Keep it in the britches I say."

The mayor walked to the edge of his truck bed.

"Sometimes, you gotta *give a crap*, so folks can *take a crap*. That's why I'm proud to sign the Go When You Please initiative in partnership with Big Ups. So every Big Rugian can relieve themselves with dignity; in the privacy of their own pants."

Folks cheered as the mayor's handlebar mustache wiggled with a smile.

"Don't believe me," he rhetorically shouted and pointed to the back of the applauding crowd. "Well, I just went *number two*…while speaking *to you*."

The audience erupted in celebration as a few folks began to chant, "Go! Go! They won't know! Number one or number two; let it pass through!"

Productivity increased all over town! Heck…that summer, I mowed lawns sun-up-to-sun-down trying to earn money for a modified short-stub bubble-muffler for my single seater. With Big Ups, I didn't see a toilet for weeks! I just kept mowing…while I was going.

Nowadays, I see Larry every Saturday morning at The Manhole. I sit at the breakfast bar and have a cup of coffee while Larry sits at the round table in the back with different business partners and investors. He's a busy guy, so we don't talk as much as we used to. But a friendship like ours doesn't need much maintenance.

My granny used to say that when you're part of someone's past, you're part of their present. Kinda like a sculptor's fingerprint hidden deep inside the clay. The outside of a vase might be smooth and flawless, but beneath the surface lie the remnants of those who helped shape it along the way.

Every now 'n again, Larry stops by Jesus Hands for a pair of gloves; and we'll spend an hour or so just talkin' 'bout the good ol' days. Boof typically breaks up the conversation, reminding us that we'd reminisce all day if left to our own devices. She's probably right, we could reminisce all day....

And if we're wearing Big Ups, we'd never need a toilet break.

The tallest mountain
        still stands on the ground.

    — *Yoderian proverb*

THE BAD JUICE DECADE

You have to be born a Fly-Down... Because you have to be born with the cat-pee-gene. It's a genetic gift, like wide nostrils or slow-growing toe nails. The cat-pee-gene alters a man's urine during adolescence, causing the urine to attract felines. Not in a reproductive way, but in a *leader of the pack* way. Fly-Downs are the lions of the alley cats!

Fly-Downs keep the zipper down on their pants for two reasons: one, it's an awesome fashion statement; two, it allows cats to better pick up on their cat-pee-gene scent.

There's nothing cooler than seeing a Fly-Down strolling through town, snapping his fingers to the rhythm of his steps. You can't miss 'em. A Fly-Down's signature look is often a black leather jacket, a white t-shirt, and tight black Levi jeans...fly down! The cuffs of the jeans are typically rolled at the ankle to show off their white socks and black dress shoes. And if a Fly-Down's greaser style isn't enough to spot him, the dozen cat's following in the wake of his footsteps is a dead giveaway... Now that's cool!

Back in the day, the Dustfog Region had three branches of Fly-Down affiliates. Big Rug's branch—the Wet Diesel Skunk Weasels—had four members. Stoolmist had two lowlifes that chartered the Golden Waters branch—a terrible name if I do say so myself—and Chigger Bottom had three brothers known as the Chigger Bottom Chaps. However, it was long disputed as to whether or not the "CBC" actually had the cat-pee-gene.

Apparently, at one point, the brothers were accused of "perfuming." That kinda accusation isn't taken lightly round these parts. Some guys spritz a little cat pee on themselves as a way of attracting a cat following to impress the ladies. It's a pathetic attempt at trying to be something they're not.

Full disclosure, I tried it once… Spritzed myself right in the eyes with cat piss. Burned like hell and gave me a rash for three days. That was the last time I ever perfumed!

At the end of the day, other towns may have Fly-Downs, but Big Rug has the cats! Trash cats are everywhere in Big Rug! Not a lot of mice, but a lot of trash, and a lot of cats. A Big Rug Fly-Down has a cat following twice the size of other Fly-Downs in the region.

Of all the Fly-Downs back in the day, Mitch was the coolest. At least in my opinion that is. But everyone had their own personal favorite. My mother always liked a Wet Diesel Skunk Weasel named Lesboken TyRell.

"Lesbo's Adam's apple beard is such a pretty shade of gray," she'd say. "Wish I was graying like that."

Lesboken was the oldest Fly-Down when I was a boy. He and Redman always sat together at The Manhole to read the paper before the sun came up. "First to read it, first to know it," they'd say to Mr. McGilbert as he'd unlock the front door in the morning.

Lesbo was in a wheelchair at a young age. He wasn't disabled, he just preferred sitting over standing. Wheelchair Lesbo was chaired-by-choice.

"Why stand when you can sit?" he'd ask while combing his Adam's apple beard. "Got me this wheelie chair right here when me great aunt passed. Haven't walked since! Savin' a bundle on shoes."

Mama was right, the man had a beautiful Adam's apple beard. His throat goat was silky-smooth and reached down to his mid-thigh. He'd tuck it into the front of his britches for church. Wheelchair Lesbo was a classy guy... No doubt!

The other two Big Rug Fly-Downs, Bibs and Jytis, were hip to the scene back in the day too. I guess they still are today... But they've never exemplified the traditional Fly-Down persona.

Bibs is buddies with my Uncle Shty. He helps test the repaired lawnmowers in my uncle's shop. Which is fine, but Bibs's white socks always have grass stains on them. I mean, don't get me wrong, Bibs is a cool dude... He wears the traditional Fly-Down black leather jacket with black Levi's; cuffs rolled up to show off his white socks and black dress shoes. But again, when the white socks are green with grass stains, it just isn't as cool.

Bibs's grass-stained socks are definitely a Fly-Down fashion faux pas, but he certainly has more style than Jytis. Jytis is a pretty boy who only wears cut off t-shirts with jean shorts...fly down! And I've never seen a guy comb his hair more than Jytis. You could have a thirty-second conversation with the man and he'd slick back his greasy hair ten times.

Aunt Sara hems his jean shorts down at her clothing store in exchange for cat hair from his cat following. She does a great job on his shorts! They have extra thick cuffs at the bottom that Jytis uses as pockets to hold his combs.

He usually has combs sticking out all the way around his thighs. He'll pull one out, slick back his hair, and toss it over his shoulder while saying, "Hair this pretty deserves a fresh comb...every time!"

Even in jean shorts, Jytis still wears the traditional black dress shoes with white socks, so at least he makes some kinda effort to celebrate his Fly-Down heritage. But it's like the guy can't tan or something... It'll be the middle of July, and he'll be whiter than a pigeon turd. The man looks like a saltine cracker dipped in bleach.

I guess cats like his white skin though, because Jytis has a huge cat following. His nickname around town is King Cat, which he has written in permanent marker on his shoulder. Drives the betties wild... At least that's what Aunt Sara says.

Nowadays, King Cat leads the yoga classes over at the old folk's home. I once watched him smack an old-timer across the face with a comb while I was visiting Grampy. Jytis whipped out a comb from his jean shorts during a downward dog stretch and smacked that geriatric fella right in the face. Jytis doesn't mess around when it comes to yoga. You better stretch that back, or you'll get a smack!

Mitch may have been the jivest Fly-Down in town, but being blessed with the cat-pee-gene still wasn't enough for that boy. Mitch had an appetite for danger! A craving for the forbidden. A sweet tooth for freshly squeezed produce juice... And in a town like Big Rug, where juicers are illegal, a sweet tooth like Mitch's will cost you a run-in with the law.

To this day, town elders still grow silent at the very mention of a time in Big Rug's history called the Bad Juice Decade. Granny and Grampy used to leave the room when Boof and I would ask questions about it.

Back when my grand folks were kids, Big Rug was a common pass-through for travelers. One day, an inventor fella passed through with a device no one in town—or anyone else in the world—had ever seen… A juicer! And as you can imagine, Big Rugians lost their minds once they tasted the sweet nectar of produce juice.

The town spiraled into a mania once folks started juicing Big Rug's Four Pillars of Nutrition: beets, pumpkin, yellow onion, and potato. The nutritional motto at the time was, "If you want a healthy body think beets for your brain, pumpkin for your stumpkin, yellow onion for the other one-ion, and potato for the rest-o." But after folks got the juice itch, the town council members changed the motto to: "Pillars must be juiced to keep fat off your caboose."

Ronny's grandfather, Mayor Lloyd Deradodo, declared juicing as the town's national past time. They even considered changing the Big Rug school mascot from the Mighty Skunk Weasels to the Fighting Juicers. The pumpkin-onion splash became the town's signature drink. Earl's Mechanic Shop and Dental Parlor stopped repairing automobiles and only repaired juicers. "Free front teeth cleaning with an auger replacement," was their advertisement at the time.

Within two years, the town of Big Rug was juicing itself dry. "The Juicing Bubble is Bound to Burst," was the frontpage headline in the *Big Rug Repository*. In the op-ed, Jerry-Jay Jerry—the town's most knowledgeable compost trader—tried warning folks about the pending juicer doom that lay ahead.

"A local economy propped up by a single commodity is only as strong as that commodity," he wrote. But folks didn't listen to Jerry-Jay Jerry's warning... Mostly because the man had baby teeth until he was in his late thirties... That's just weird. It's hard to take advice from a grown man with baby teeth.

So, although Jerry-Jay Jerry warned against it, folks continued to cut loose with a little juicer juice. All day, every day, they juiced their lives away. The day the juice hit the fan—and the local economy hit the floor—was when The Big Rug Bank started mortgaging juicers. After that, things got really bad, really fast.

Within two years, Big Rug had twenty juicers to every one Big Rugian. The town was so heavily littered with juicer parts that it looked like the soil was growing metal screws instead of grass. Tyrannosaurus-Wrecks & Scrapodon Yard overflowed with rind, creating a stench in the air so foul that people had to wear bandanas over their faces when stepping outside.

Many folks became ill with something called Fat Lip. The acidity of certain juice blends caused an allergic reaction, resulting in the swelling of a person's top lip and restricting their ability to breathe through their nose.

Fat Lip was a major health concern, but it only impacted a portion of the town. The Juicer Howl, on the other hand, tortured everyone. The constant buzzing of juicers drowned out all other sounds around town. Folks' voices went hoarse trying to yell over the noise. Some went crazy, screaming in the streets while covering their ears from the Juicer Howl.

In a fit of desperation, the newly-appointed sheriff at the time, Barney Beitzel—Sheriff Shitzel's great-uncle—gathered the town's men and a pack of bloodhounds to put an end to the juicer madness. That cold, dark evening would later be known as The Midnight Rage.

The men searched and seized every last juicer in town, exorcising Big Rugians of the mechanical demons that haunted them. They dug up all the caskets in the Big Rug Cemetery and Pee-Wee Football Field, removed the bodies inside, and buried the juicers in their place.

And as the last shovel spread dirt across the burial ground, the sun rose from the east once more; giving light to a town that had become all too familiar with the dark. Barney Beitzel, and his band of brothers, had successfully purged the town of Big Rug from its juicer madness.

The National Guard and FEMA were called into town pretty quickly after The Midnight Rage because of all the carcasses sitting above ground. Federal authorities condemned Big Rug for three weeks due to the flies and wild animals that the decomposing bodies attracted. But… the juicers were defeated!

Fat Lip virtually disappeared overnight, and the Juicer Howl was vanquished back to the depths of hell from which it came… And, despite the unearthing of the Big Rug Cemetery and Pee-Wee Football Field during The Midnight Rage, not a single pee-wee football game was canceled. In this town, whether it's rain or shine, snow or sleet, rocks or the brittle carcasses of the deceased littering the field…the game goes on!

Mayor Lloyd Deradodo signed legislation banning juicers from the town of Big Rug. Punishment for being caught, *"In the possession of juice; and/or in the possession of a juicer or juicer parts, trying to build a juicer, or purchasing a juicer,"* was a minimum sentence of eight months in jail.

Truth be told, the town has never really enforced the "juice" part of the law. It's the "juicer" that has the mark of the beast. And rightfully so. To this day, you can't dig a hole in the soil of Big Rug without finding a rusty spring or screw from the Bad Juice Decade.

A few years after I was born, Hank Deradodo organized a protest at the Clowns Don't Frown Culinary Arts Institute and marched the crowd to city hall where they forced his younger brother—Mayor Billy-Boy Deradodo—to adjust the sentence from eight months in jail, to eight days of community service. But the mayor stood firm on the "no juicers of any kind" policy; which includes educational facilities like the CDFCAI.

"Family don't erase history, Hank!" Billy-Boy argued while trying to calm his younger brother's protest. "Juice let loose leads to abuse. Learned that lesson once… Don't need to learn it twice. This town remembers The Midnight Rage. May been 'a boy back when the madness came to town, but I still hear juicers howling in my dreams!"

"Bill…that's unreasonable," Hank pleaded. "The Clowns Don't Frown Culinary Arts Institute has a reputation to uphold. Who's gonna take us seriously without a juicing curriculum? You just had a baby boy a few months ago, Bill… You want baby Ronny to grow up in a town that's laughed at by the culinary community?"

"You wanna see a clown frown, do ya?" the mayor yelled looking around at the folks gathered outside city hall, his eyes watering with rage. "Put a juicer in their hands! Then you'll see a clown frown! Hard to smile with Fat Lip! Mother got Fat Lip, Hank… Remember that? Her top lip got fat as a hot dog and pink as a skunk weasel's ass."

A tear rolled down Billy-Boy's cheek and disappeared into his handlebar mustache.

"Papa had to drain it twice a day with a hot needle," his voice cracked as he threw his cowboy hat to the ground. "All from the juice damn it! Now, any y'all folks *cruisin' for a juicin'*...you can cruise right on outta town and into Plumpstin City. Them city folks wanna live on the edge of morality, they can suffer the consequences."

The two brothers argued back and forth all afternoon on the steps of town hall, but the mayor wouldn't budge.

"The Devil's drink ain't flowin' through this town ever again! No juicers in Big Rug... Period!"

The argument got so heated that Hank threatened to move the Clowns Don't Frown Culinary Arts Institute out west near Mumper. Thank the good Lord he didn't though. Big Rug just wouldn't have the same refinement without a regionally recognized higher education academy like the CDFCAI. It's just like my grampy used to say, "Havin' the smarts, or havin' the farts...both will get your attention."

Not sure if I mentioned this, but my cousin Fannie graduated from the CDFCAI with almost a B average... So, yeah...education is pretty important in my family!

I mean, Cousin Fannie can cook pancakes in the shape of freakin' balloons! And...I've yet to meet someone who went to one of those fancy four-year degree state schools who can ride a tiny bicycle in oversized plastic red shoes... Nuff said!

Mitch's grandfather owned Earl's Mechanic Shop and Dental Parlor, which later became Sek-C's Auto Body Shop when Mitch's father took over and eliminated the dental services. "Ain't enough teeth in town for dental stuff," Mitch's father told me.

Growing up in a family of mechanics gave Mitch the ability to build just about anything. And he was particularly skilled at fashioning together makeshift juicers out of automotive parts to create some of the best beverages us boys had ever drank. In the cover of night, the boys and I would head over to Sek-C's Auto Body Shop to delight in Mitch's latest juicing creations. It was risky, but sometimes the juice is worth the squeeze.

Every three months or so, Shiffy and the sheriff would pull into Sek-C's with their lights flashing to confiscate Mitch's juicers. His eight days of community service was always trimming the crepe myrtles at the Lumberjack Training Yard. Things went on like that for years. And each year that passed, Mitch's patience grew smaller as his dreams of juicing grew bigger.

I knew Mitch was reaching his tipping point on his seventeenth birthday. That morning Mitch, Brant, and I headed to Dust Fog Market to pick up some fresh produce for the birthday party later that night.

"Keep your eyes open for banana peppers," Mitch reminded us as we weaved through the aisles of the outdoor market.

If you head south out of town toward Chigger Bottom, you run into Dust Fog Market, the farmers co-op for the Dustfog Region. All the towns have a section identified by flags where they sell food and specialty items.

Low Water's flag is white, and dons the Ormish hex sign of the frog-dragon. Mumper's flag is black with an orange pumpkin in the top left corner and Chigger Bottom's is white with a piece of coal in the corner. Plumpstin City's flag is maroon with a yellow six-pointed star in the center of the flag representing the six municipalities of the Dustfog Region.

Big Rug's flag is a classic brown corduroy flag. Folks like to spice it up by hooking fishing lures on it though... The flag really sparkles on a bright sunny day.

Last, and definitely least, Stoolmist has a total piece of crap flag that's so ugly it's borderline offensive. It's gold and green and has some other stupid stuff on it like you'd expect from them grumper-bumpers. I'd rather look at Sheriff Beitzel's double bellybutton than that ugly flag.

Dust Fog Market has all kinds of great stuff. Folks from Big Rug mostly sell potatoes and bags of pollen. It's our niche. The bags of pollen aren't great sellers though. I've never understood why. Seems to me if you can bag it, you should be able to sell it! Folks bag and sell dirt. Folks bag and sell rocks. I've seen folks bag and sell just about everything.

Years back, I had to do some traveling to pick up a truck for my wife's birthday. While traveling, I saw a fella picking up—and bagging—dog dirt. "Officer Scooper, *the Pet Waste Trooper!*" is what it said on the side of his truck. I'm inclined to believe Officer Scooper was then selling those bags of dog dirt for a hefty profit. But, I'm no expert in the dog dirt business...

I know a thing or two about the profit margins of cow crap though. I even know a little bit about donkey droppings. But dog dirt, that's a refined man's game. A connoisseur of manure if you will...

There are hundreds of varieties. Which is why in the compost community, dog dirt is considered to be the "red wine" of manure.

"Look gents," I heard Preston's stupid voice from across the aisle. "Big Rug must'a farted and squirted out three turds."

Hudson cackled like a buck-toothed hyena, "I knew you ditch-donkeys were close. I could smell Brant from across the market."

"Yeah Brant. It's one thing to have school spirit, but actually smelling like an ass weasel is just pathetic," Stinkin' Lincoln mocked while slapping Oliver a high-five.

"It's *skunk weasel*, you no good Ferry Flower," I fumed. "And you look like a fat-headed tad pole, Stincoln!"

"Yawp," Brant barked.

"A fat-headed tad pole..." Mitch stepped forward like a totally awesome dude. "More like a hot air balloon with hair," he smirked, popping the collar of his black leather jacket. "And Hudson...your buck teeth are so big, they reflect the sun."

"Overbites are a serious medical condition," Hudson shouted.

"Your breath is a serious medical condition," Mitch replied.

"Ahhh," Hudson scoffed and waved his hands. "Go kiss a cat, you Fly-Down wagon wheel."

Mitch laughed. "I'll kiss your mom, Hudson. On the lips! And then I'll take the Love Walk and marry her so I'll be your stepdad; and you'll have to call me sir!"

Fat Neck Oliver stepped around a vegetable cart and shouted, "*Big Dumbians* can't lumberjack."

I quickly responded, "*Buttmisters* can't farm!"

"No." He tossed a lettuce leaf at me. "*You* can't farm."

I yelled back, "You'll never grow a throat goat Oliver! You have lady skin on your fat neck!"

"You don't know jack squat," he screamed in my face, causing Redman to pop up from a pigeon liver cart and scold us right there in the middle of Dust Fog Market, in front of everyone, including a few betties.

Redman threw his hands in the air and kicked a lettuce leaf littering the ground.

"Shut your chip 'n chirpin'! Adam's apple beards and the lady skin... Foul mouthed hooters. Dang black-billed cuckoo's makin' a ruckus... *Nope!* Not in my day... I tell you, shoots... Just like yat you do... Just... Like... Yat!"

The old man softened his tone and mumbled, "Bunch 'a wondering albatross I say you are... Who's a whose who? Who. Is. A. Whose. Who?"

He threw a handful of banana peppers at us before stomping away and yelling, "Get a job!"

Redman's rant scared off the Ferry Flowers but not before we all passed a few parting insults under our breath. They went back to shopping for lady's underwear—I'm assuming that's what they were shopping for—and we went back to shopping for Mitch's birthday party produce.

"Found the banana peppers," Brant laughed.

The night of Mitch's seventeenth birthday, we headed to Sek-C's to let loose with a little juicer juice. And to my surprise, quite a few people showed up. Suzie LaCuzzi stopped by, the Zapinsky sisters, Marie-Agnus and Big Rig Bevy. Heck, even Boof and her best friend Tippin' Tilda made an appearance.

Tilda's right leg was a few inches shorter than her left, so it looked like she was tipping over; hence the nickname, Tippin' Tilda. Sometimes, she'd duct tape a Webster's dictionary under her right shoe to even things out.

The evening began heating up when Mitch and Dale started juicing hard on hot-tarties. At one point, they juiced an entire lemon—shaved and soaked in Ormish hooch—with a splash of tabasco sauce. And, both of them knocked it back in one shot... I can still hear Mitch's gulp rattling through the garage as his neck widened to swallow the shot.

"Who's next?" he coughed, holding up a lemon and a bottle of tabasco sauce.

"We'll take one," Andrea chimed while downing a shot with her sister Haley.

"Holy hot-tarty," Haley coughed with a smile. "That has a little zip to it!"

Tippin' Tilda stomped her dictionary shoe in anger and shouted, "Are you people crazy? I won't be part of this. It's too much," she insisted while teeter tottering frantically around the garage and gathering her things.

"Dictionary came off your shoe," Larry loudly announced holding the book up by a strand of duct tape.

"Y'all don't even know..." Tilda said with tears in her eyes. "I used to baby sit these two sweet girls. One night, their dad lost his job and drowned his sorrows in hot-tarties.

He made three shots, one for each year on the job. He took one shot and immediately passed out from heat-gut. It's a real thing y'all... Look it up in my shoe," she pointed at Larry.

"The two girls found the other shots sitting on the kitchen table and drank them," she wailed while wiping a tear from her eye. "*And they died!* The Huggabee sisters are dead from hot-tarties. It melted their insides like popsicles in an oven!"

"I heard the same thing at school," Larry added. "Heard the Huggabees looked like half-filled water balloons when their mom found them. Even their skeletons melted…Sheriff Shitzel's wristwatch got snagged and popped one of the girls while putting their water-bodies in the ambulance."

"Skin balloons," Ronny whispered, taking off his stocking cap to show respect as the garage grew silent.

"Those poor dead Huggabees deserved better," Tilda whimpered, stepping on an oil can to straighten herself out. "And it's disrespectful to be juicing hot-tarties while people are still grieving," she continued scolding us as we shamefully lowered our heads, saddened by the death of our classmates.

Our moment of remembrance only lasted for a few seconds before Haley and Andrea scared the bejesus out of us by screeching, "Our mother remarried! We are the Huggabees! What is wrong with you people?"

The sisters stormed out in offense, leaving us in shock. Tippin' Tilda sniffled and wiped her face dry.

"Wait," she muttered looking around embarrassed. "Didn't one of them used to wear a back brace?"

"Tattoos!" Mitch stood up interrupting the awkwardness. "Let's get tattoos!"

And just like that, we were walking in the door of Pterodac-toos, *"Two Toe-toos for the Price of One!"*

When we entered the tattoo parlor, we found Coach, lying face down, getting an outline of Europe tattooed on his lower back.

"It's European," Coach bragged looking up at us. "Big city stuff boys... No one in Big Rug got this! Europe a country. Y'all don't know nothin' 'bout no foreigns."

"Why's it so small?" Ronny asked while squinting and adjusting his glasses. "It kinda looks like a strange mole."

"That's how it's s'pposed to be. It's big city stuff! Learn a book," Coach snapped, ungracefully sliding his whistle into his mouth and quickly chirping it twice. "Dismissed!"

Mitch walked out of Pterodac-toos with a stainless-steel juicer inked on his forearm for all the world to see.

When folks around town saw his tattoo, they'd whisper and scoff. One day at The Manhole, Redman got so mad that he threw a piece of toast at Mitch.

"Star-crossed juicin' jerk... Jive turkey vulture 'n the Fly-Down cat-pee-gene nonsense... Juicin' too-toos! Too-Toos I tell ya... *Nope!* Not in my day... I tell you, shoots!"

The disapproval of others never bothered Mitch though. He knew what he liked, regardless of what others thought.

But how long can a lion live with hyenas before being consumed by the pack? Before being forced to choose; stay to die, or leave alive? It's just like my grampy used to say, "A fish outta water can never find a home."

Mitch chased his dream of the perfect juice blend for as long as I knew him. And it was chasing that dream that ultimately led him out of the town of Big Rug. He simply deserved more than this town could offer. He knew it, and the rest of us knew it too.

Mitch deserved a pressure pressed wheat grass chiller with a thinly sliced cucumber sitting on a cured honey glass rim. Not a pumpkin-onion splash with a hint of motor grease from whatever automotive parts he'd pieced together to build a juicer.

One summer's eve, just a few weeks after Mitch's birthday, I headed to Sek-C's to meet him for a beet juice blast. It was quiet as a moosemunk when I pulled up, which was strange, considering Mitch was expecting me. All the lights were off but one lamp shining in the back of the garage by the indoor porta potty. I walked back to give Mitch a good scare, but he was nowhere to be found.

"Mitch…" I shouted to a silent reply.

I meandered in the silence of the shop, softly touching tools and gadgets as I passed. I could hear a train rumbling through town off in the distance, and in that moment, I felt deeply alone. As if I was the only person on Earth. There was no motorbike, no cats, and no Mitch anywhere to be seen. An empty world, but for me.

The setting sun shining through the windows caught my eye as the dusty air glistened in the downward streaking light. I stared at the sharpness of the soft yellow sunrays for a moment before noticing a fresh glass of beet juice blast sitting on the countertop. Beside it was a folded note that read,

> "To the boys,
>   I'll never make a drink as special as you, but I have to try.
>   – Mitch"

I stepped out the front door in disbelief, taking off my ballcap as I looked side-to-side for signs of my friend. I walked to the edge of the gravel driveway, looking down into the twilight of the setting sun, as if peering into the emptiness I felt deep inside my chest.

A butterfly flew into my view, catching my attention and serving as a distraction from a friend's farewell. I watched it flutter its large wings, gently hopping across the air. In and out of the shadows, in and out of the light; dancing through the colors of an endless world. Floating in the buzz of a summer's sunset, far from the buzz of a juicer.

Maybe that's what life is, for most of us? A colorful confusion. And we, like a butterfly, are floating in and out of the shadows, searching for direction in an open space; for shelter to rest our wings in the never-ending struggle to stay afloat.

Maybe that's what Mitch really wanted. A life with direction. A life with purpose. I guess he decided the first step in finding his purpose was jumping on his motorbike and riding through the open space in a single direction, hoping to find shelter in the never-ending struggle of life.

I don't know if Mitch turned east or west when riding out of Sek-C's Auto Body Shop. I don't know how he chose his direction in an open space... I don't know if he knew his destination, if he packed a bag, or if he kissed his mother goodbye. I don't know much about that summer's eve. But I like to think that Mitch turned into the sunset, riding toward the light and not toward the darkness.

I imagine the silhouette of a boy on his motorbike, racing out of Big Rug and into the setting sun. Chasing down a dream with a head full of steam. Finding *his* direction, pursuing *his* purpose. Riding into *his* future and out of *his* past. A black leather jacket and a bike full of gas... Fly down!

All are blind with shut eyes.

— Ormish scripture

THE TICKLE MONSTER

Gus may not have been a stud muffin like Larry, but he was definitely a country hunk! And the boy was tough! Yes, his elbows had dimples… But man-o-live could Gus chop a block!

"It's all in the hips," he'd say, splitting a chop block with a single swing of his axe.

After a successful chop, he'd take his jerky stick out of his mouth and tap it like he was ashing a cigar.

"Beef Cigar," he'd boast pushing up his brown chubby cheeks with a smile.

Gus was just a different kinda guy. He always had food in his pockets. I don't mean food in a wrapper or something, I mean handfuls of trail mix in his trouser pockets. Or crunched up potato chips mixed with pocket lint.

"Why don't you just put the food in a bag," Chad always complained in disgust.

"My britches are clean," Gus would argue while reaching in his pockets for a snack.

Gus—in all his oddities—had a way of changing how the boys and I viewed the world. I remember in fourth grade, Gus asked Mrs. Boil why we pronounce W, "double-U", when it's really a "double-V." It was the first time I saw a teacher speechless. And one time, he asked Miss Grittle why "fat chance" and "slim chance" mean the same thing.

To this day, I still wonder why a boxing ring is square, or why we call a piano player a pianist, but we don't call a race car driver a racist? And why the heck isn't eleven, twelve, thirteen and fifteen pronounced oneteen, twoteen, threeteen, and fiveteen? If not for Gus, I would've never asked myself these questions.

Gus lived next door to me as a kid. Our fathers grew up together, and our mothers are cousins. Our parents were basically inseparable. But our fathers took it to another level. Mama said they might as well be one person. She even gave them a nickname by combining Phil and Dewey to create "Phewey."

"Phewey and the half brains," she'd tease when they'd do something silly.

When I was in third grade, we had a bad storm that swept through the Dustfog Region, forcing folks to shelter in place for fifteen days. The superstorm roared while shooting bolts of lightning from its dark clouds in fits of rage as it fought to pass over Mrs. Yoder's Mountain.

I was certain the storm meant something special was happening. Like I was living through one of God's Great Storms on Mrs. Yoder's Mountain that birthed the Ormish Oak. A few days after the storm, I was walking home from Brant's house and I swear I saw a cotton-haired mule with wings; reinforcing my theory that the storm was a supernatural event. But now, as an adult, I'm pretty sure it was just a cotton-haired mule in a thermal cow coat.

Although no mythical beings were born from the storm, it did blow over an elm tree in Gus's back yard, creating a giant hole from the tree's root base. It looked like the ground had a big lid that was opened halfway. With the help of our fathers, Gus and I built an underground fort large enough to comfortably seat all the boys.

Uncle Shty and Coach hung out down there too. Coach put a welcome rug at the entrance.

"Ain't gettin' these sneakers dirty," Coach complained. "These multi-sport sneakers. Big city stuff. Can't get these sneakers round here. Only sell 'em in the city!"

It only took a few months before the fort collapsed from erosion. To be honest, Pops was more upset than I was. The morning after it collapsed, Pops threw his hands in the air and yelled, "Welp, there goes twenty bucks in lumber!"

"Dewey," Mama sighed. "You and Phil can sit above ground and drink beer like normal people."

"I'm diggin' it out Trishy-Sue," Pops yelled with tears in his eyes. "And I'm puttin' a lazy-boy recliner down there! Like I should've done the first time!"

The following Monday, Gus was sitting next to the porta potty outside the entrance of our school with a cardboard sign that read, *"Mud Scrubs! 2 ¢. Betties Only."*

He'd collected mud from the collapsed fort and was offering foot scrubs to the girls as they walked into school. You almost have to admire that kinda entrepreneurial spirit.

But it was still pretty weird. The girls thought so too. The only "betties" who took part in the foot scrubs were Lunch Lady Irwin and Principal Keck.

Gus may have been an odd boy, but no one messed with that jelly belly. Except for us boys of course... And we knew just how to get him shakin' in his boots, the Tickle Monster! Gus was terrified of the Tickle Monster.

Earl refers to the Tickle Monster as the North American Sloth. He even sketched some pictures of the creature and super glued them in the encyclopedia down at the Big Rug Magazine Library and Coupon Trading Post. Some folks say the Tickle Monster is an urban legend. An old wives' tale meant to give kids the willies. But if it's in the encyclopedia...it has to be true!

"The Tickle Monster is the Loch Ness Monster of Big Rug," Preacher Jepp told us back in Sunday school.

He knelt down on one knee to get closer to the group of children sitting Ormish style on the rug.

"It's fake! Like wheat-worms in your cereal. Trust me, there were no Tickle Monsters on Noah's ark, and there are no Tickle Monsters in Big Rug."

Preacher Jepp wasn't alone in his disbelief. There's a lot of Tickle Monster skepticism out there. But as for Gus...he believes! And so do most Big Rugians. Heck, I'd be lying like a llama wearing lipstick if I said I didn't sleep with a jar of honey by my bed as a kid to ward off the Tickle Monster.

Tickle Monsters love sweets and can't resist the temptation of a sugary snack. If you sleep with an open jar of honey by your bed, a Tickle Monster can't resist dipping its feathery fingers in for a taste. The honey gums up its feathers, neutralizing its ability to tickle.

Pops used to wiggle his fingers in a tickling motion while tucking Boof and I into bed and say, "Put honey by your bed, so you wake up undead."

The only other thing that protects children from the Tickle Monster is a snoring mother…and only a snoring mother will do. No other type of person snoring has the right frequency to deter the Tickle Monster.

Around these parts, we call snoring mothers the Angels of Big Rug… Big Rugian women saws logs like a sedated bison. Big time throat throttles. Gals round these parts snore like they're trying to vibrate the rafters. The first time I heard Brekanny jackhammer her sinuses, I knew she'd be the future mother of my children.

When Gus was a kid, he overheard a conversation the morning after his grandfather passed away. Gus was listening from the hallway and heard his mother say, "He peed himself. I knew something was wrong when I saw the wet sheets."

"Pap-Pap was tickled to death," Gus told us boys the next day. "Everyone knows when the Tickle Monster gets ya, you laugh so hard you pee… And then you die! There's no other explanation. The Tickle Monster got Pap-Pap… The proof is in the piss!"

When they found Gus's grandfather, he not only peed himself, but he also went number two. So, he must've been laughing *really, really* hard! But there's no shame in a chuckle truffle. I've personally never pinched a loaf while laughing, but I've let out a warning call a time or two. Gas laughs run in my family.

Aunt Sara's a hard laugher… She carries an extra pair of undies in her purse, "just in case." We buy her Big Ups every year for her birthday, but she's a traditional kinda gal. You know Aunt Sara's wearing one of her lady thongs when she's laughing so hard that she says, "I'm 'a 'bout to split a log." Usually, she just gets a case of the tinkles though…

But again, she refuses to wear Big Ups like a civilized person. So, she just walks around town in her pee jeans. "Sara's got her pee jeans on," folks say.

Children all across Big Rug lay awake at night for fear of falling asleep, only to be woken up by the Tickle Monster tickling their toes. The Tickle Monster doesn't tickle tiny toes for pleasure though, it tickles for survival.

Tickle Monsters are silent beasts, unable to chip, chirp, or roar. While other animals rely on their own vocal abilities to communicate, Tickle Monsters howl through the sound of laughing children. Their young victims—resting in their slumber—laugh so hard that they die from the giggles. It's tragic...

Most folks believe that the Tickle Monster living in the Dust Fog Region is calling out to a long-lost love. A mate that he was somehow separated from. It has been said that the only cure for the Tickle Monster's loneliness is to reunite with his long-lost love. Unfortunately, in the case of the Tickle Monster...love kills! But the dead always leave with a smile on their face.

Growing up, if Boof and I ever saw a pee-stained sheet hanging on a clothesline, we knew exactly what happened. The Tickle Monster got 'em! There was a poem about the Tickle Monster that Granny used to read us as kids:

> *"If you sit in silence, you'll hear the delight,*
> *of sleeping children, laughing in fright,*
> *as the Tickle Monster tickles, in the dead of the night."*

Whoowa... Even today, it gives me the heebie-jeebies just thinkin' 'bout it.

In the fifth grade, the Tickle Monster chatter got so bad that Mayor Deradodo had to call a town meeting in the barning-barn behind the Big Rug High School and Brush Burn Yard. It was the first time I'd been in the newly built barning-barn.

"If we wish to barn, then we must build a barn, so we may learn to barn." our barning teacher, Mr. Brofen, proclaimed through his walrus mustache.

Barning's an advanced placement class here in Big Rug. If a student is exceptional in kindergardening and can ace integrated mulching through elementary school, then freshman and sophomore year, they can take compost theory, hay stacking, hay baling, and hay flooring. If a child excels in those classes, they can apply for acceptance into barning fundamentals their junior year.

Boof took barning fundamentals and loved it! I almost had to repeat kindergardening, so I didn't have a chance. Dang shovel theory always tripped me up. I still get confused on when to use a spade shovel or a round point shovel.

When my family walked into the Tickle Monster meeting, I saw Brant's dad, Earl, on the elevated stage of the large barn room preparing to address the crowd. Seemed like the whole dang town was squeezed inside the barning-barn. Pops was leading us through the crowd when out of nowhere, he spotted Gus's dad and made a beeline straight to him, abandoning Mama, Boof, and me.

"Thanks for waiting for us," Mama reamed my father once we found him.

"First come, first serve," Pops smiled. "I saved you seats."

"Where's Gus?" Mama asked Phil while situating herself in a folding chair.

"Don't know. Lost 'em in the crowd I guess?" he replied, arching his back to get a better view of Earl.

"Hey there folks. I've called this meeting at Mayor Billy-Boy Deradodo's request," Earl informed the uneasy crowd while shuffling through a few notecards. "With a little information, maybe we can calm the Tickle Monster worry around town.

"Let me start by asking those of you in the crowd who are of the Fly-Down persuasion, please, if possibly, try to control your feline following. At our last meeting, several folks reported instances of cats regurgitating hairballs under their seats, or on their feet."

"And I was wearing flip flops," Aunt Sara complained.

"Bring out Bozo Goober," some high school kid hollered from the back.

"The Goob," a few betties shouted. "Woo-hoo…"

"No, no…no," Earl looked up. "Bozo Goober and the Spoons in the Spotlight are not performing at this meeting. That was just a rumor spreading around town," he explained as the group of kids exited the barning-barn in disappointment.

"As I was saying," Earl continued while placing his forest ranger's hat on the podium and running his fingers through his thick red hair. "The North American sloth, or as some folks call it, the Tickle Monster, is a slow-moving, nocturnal, pinecone-eating mammal. Many believe the North American sloth is a relative of the brown-throated sloth found in the forest of South America."

Earl gestured to a large sketch resting on an easel to his left and said, "Pucker Loaf was kind enough to render this drawing of the North American sloth for our discussion tonight. I hope his artistic hand, accompanied with a few facts about the creature, can help us better understand exactly what it is we're dealing with."

"These here floors of this here barn," Mr. Brofen interrupted from his seat, "came from reclaimed Highgrass golden cedar… From one of the original bridges of Low Water," he bubbled, joyfully looking around the room.

Earl, somewhat confused by Mr. Brofen's interruption, continued his presentation.

"The North American sloth is a solitary tree-dwelling animal; weighing around ten pounds with short hind legs and long arms to climb… And to tickle. The creature's short, hairless snout exposes its dark skin and upward curling mouth, giving the appearance of a friendly smile."

Earl paused and lowered his eyeglasses. He stepped out from behind the podium and raised both hands in a plea to the crowd.

"But I'm asking all of you, *please* do not approach this animal! Although friendly looking, we still don't know the risk of approaching a North American sloth in the wild."

Through the silence of the crowd, Uncle Shty yelled from somewhere behind me, "Shoot 'em on sight."

"With all this I've said," Earl proceeded, returning to the podium and ignoring Uncle Shty's outburst, "the most unique identifier is its long, down-like feathers at the tips of its fingers. The feathers can be up to sixteen inches long and shed biannually.

"In other words, the creature's finger-feathers have an incredible ability to maintain their purity; keeping free from debris and other contaminants that might compromise their softness. These remarkable features make the North American sloth the greatest tickling species on Earth!"

The crowd gasped as murmurs filled the barning barn.

"Remarkable...?" Chad's mother stood up offended while protectively palming Chad's head against her thigh. "Earl...? Children aren't safe."

"Darcey-Dee..." Markio softly scolded. "Sit... Down... You ain't wearin' no bra woman."

Mr. McGilbert stood up and sighed. "My girls piss the bed every night, Earl," he groaned and pointed down at his blushing daughters. "They're thirteen damn it!"

"It's the Tickle Monster," Jytis yelled and pulled out a comb from his hemmed jean shorts. "Folks all the way from Bewster Grove to Chigger Bottom sayin' they hearin' kids laughin' in the night," he informed the crowd while slicking back his hair and winking at Lunch Lady Irwin.

"These here windows of this here barn," the pudgy Mr. Brofen gleefully interrupted like some kinda lumberjack-looking Santy Claus, "were installed by myself and two young fellers from Chigger Bottom... Nice young fellers. Now...you might think we used two-inch nails for the windows. But," his chubby cheeks blushed with excitement, "we actually used these here one-and-a-half-inch galvanized roofing nails. And here's why, the pinewood..."

"Cut down the blue spruces," Mr. McGilbert shouted at Earl.

"Make the bet and I'll get wet," I heard Chad yell from his seat.

"Easy everyone," our science teacher implored. "We've only heard rumors that the Tickle Mon...," he quickly paused and cleared his throat. "Excuse me… That the *North American sloth*," he looked up at Earl and nodded, "lives under blue spruces. But there's no scientific evidence to confirm this belief."

"Science for the witches," a woman yelled through one of the open windows.

"Yawp," Brant's voice belted through the barn from the rafters.

A restlessness began to roll through the crowd as Mr. Stoltzer sighed, shaking his head in disappointment.

"Until someone has the courage to climb inside the bottom of a blue spruce, we can't just go around town cutting down the forest based on hearsay."

"Sit down four-eyes," Sheriff Beitzel blurted from the front row, grinning and looking around for a laugh. "Cause he wears glasses," he mumbled to the old lady sitting next to him.

"See na see," Muhck raised his voice. "Me 'n Mimi made a special science trap for the Tickle Monster. Filled it with toenail clippings. Science say Tickle Monsters love the scent of toenails."

"Muhck! Dang it to hell," Coach whined. "Science say they has to be *fresh* toenails," he asserted while winking at our science teacher, as if he was helping Mr. Stoltzer in some way.

"Dismissed," Coach chirped his whistle.

"Fresh or clipped, they still has to be little kid toenails," Sheriff Beitzel said. "Tickle Monsters love little kid toenails."

The sheriff sat back in his chair and pulled a tinfoil wrapped double-onion-coney-dog from his jacket. Which quickly caught the eye of my Aunt Sara. Her big head popped up outta the crowd like a saddle-dog sniffin' a porkshroud.

"Um… Excuse me…" Aunt Sara complained and raised her hand. "Excuse me, Earl… Okay, I'm not trying to be rude here, but, I was under the impression that there'd be finger food at this meeting. And as far as I can see, there ain't even refreshments. I had a light dinner, Earl… Assuming there'd be snacks."

"Look at what happened to the Huggabee girls," Lunch Lady Irwin cried.

Her petite frame, and thick yellow onion hair, rose from the center seats in a white V-neck low enough to touch her belt buckle. She briefly batted her eyes at Jytis and provocatively adjusted her blouse while pouting her bottom lip.

"They've disappeared," she pouted. "The Tickle Monster got them. I just know it!"

The folks around me whispered back and forth as the crowd grew anxious.

"The Huggabee's were tickled to death?" I heard someone say.

"Oh, my word," the woman behind me murmured. "I knew the Huggabees died, but I didn't know how."

Lunch lady Irwin wailed, "Those sweet girls are dead, Earl."

"Tickle Monster got 'em with his silly little feather fingers," Coach insisted. "Big city police gots the SWATs for monsters. Fight 'em... Likeyat," he grunted and kicked his foot in the air.

Sheriff Beitzel leapt from his seat, accidentally knocking the elderly woman sitting beside him to the ground.

"Huggabees died in the hailstorm last year... And that's a fact. Overheard it while eating lunch at Meat-a-Tatoes! Icy rain is what killed them girls," he demanded while shoving the last bite of his coney-dog into his mouth.

"Our mother remarried," Haley screamed while jumping up from her seat in a tantrum.

"Miss Zapinsky," snapped Principal Keck from the side of the room, motioning for Haley to sit down. "Now is not the time to seek attention," she silently mouthed.

"It's true," Principal Keck affirmed while adjusting her stonewashed denim pant suit. "The Huggabee sisters are no longer on the school roster. Their names disappeared from the roster over the summer. I overheard a few girls gossiping in the porta potty outside the Don't Drink Paint Supply entrance. It seems the rumors are true… The Tickle Monster killed the Huggabees!"

Mayor Deradodo walked to the edge of the wooden stage, sensing the uneasiness of the crowd. "Thank ya Principal Keck. That'll be 'a nuff. Friends, I assure ya. We're takin' every precaution in keepin' a safe community."

"It's those sexual deviants from the city," Miss Poterspeel crowed while waving her crooked finger in the air. "They use feathers for their perverted devil worship stuff," she said while clutching her purse. "I heard it on the radio! The women wear shoes made for men. That's how you know they're perverts."

"Garbage eatin' seagulls," Redman gripped. "City pre-verts ticklin' kiddie toes… *Nope!* Not in my day… I tell you, shoots…"

Through the crowd I could see Dr. Plakas helping the old lady that Sheriff Beitzel had knocked over.

"Billy-Boy… Sir," he said, placing the old lady back into her seat. "Why don't you have the sheriff climb his fat butt under the blue spruces in town and look for a Tickle Monster nest?"

"Good idea!" several folks grumbled. "Send the sheriff!"

"Too dangerous friends," the mayor responded.

"Dr. Plakas, was ya not the one who put these here bandages over my ears just last night?"

"Well…yes," Dr. Plakas politely replied.

"And how'd I injure my ears?" the mayor asked softly.

"Trying to climb under a blue spruce," Dr. Plakas mumbled and lowered his head.

"Tryin' to climb...under a spruce..." the mayor gently repeated.

He paused with a smile and scanned the room; making eye contact with folks as he peered across the crowd. The mayor knew what he was doing... He was intentionally calming the crowd; setting us up for what was coming next.

"Pine needles!" Mayor Deradodo shouted, smacking his hands together with a *crack* and startling the crowd. "Right to my ears! Punctured both eardrums!"

The old lady that Dr. Plakas had just helped back into her seat, fainted from the scare, and tumbled back to the floor.

"Wasn't me..." Sheriff Beitzel insisted.

"Fine folks down in Chigger Bottom sending up all the honey jars they can," the mayor continued. "One jar per household they sayin'. Stop by the office if ya'd like one. Chiggarians and Big Rugians workin' together folks. Put an end to this Tickle Monster nonsense.

"Friends, I know the first thing ya think when a child wets the bed... A Tickle Monster got 'em!" he called out, waving his hands.

"One time," Wheelchair Lesbo passionately recalled from the front row, "when I's a boy, I heard a loud moaning coming from me mother's room. It woke me slumber. When I peeked in the door, I saw a beast with two backs rolling on the bed... Eating a pillow or something? Had a tattoo of a slice of cheese on its shoulder... Just like me mama had," Lesbo shouted and smacked the armrest of his wheelchair.

"Why ain't nobody talkin' 'bout them grass ghosts?" Mr. Neff interjected in a frustrated outburst.

"Ya," a few men agreed.

"Ain't he a homo with Petey-Parv Pritchet?" I heard someone whisper from the row behind me.

"Shoot 'em on sight," Uncle Shty yelled.

"Cornbread cornbread," Cornbread vented and shook his fist.

Mama whispered in my father's ear, "Grass ghosts…?"

"Ya… Grass ghosts…. The collective grass clippings of mowed lawns; risen from the dead, to wreak havoc on your lawn."

"See na see," Muhck snorted and stood up on his seat. "Them grass ghost the reason for all the weeds round town!"

"Damn right," Mr. Neff replied. "I ain't mowing my yard until the grass ghosts in this town are dealt with!"

Through the crowd, I could see Mrs. Neff looking over her shoulder at my mother and rolling her eyes.

"There's no point in mowing," Mr. Neff continued. "The more we mow, the stronger they get! Before we know it, the grass ghosts will have this whole dang town buried in weeds."

"Ya!" Pops yelled unexpectedly, frightening my mother and eliciting a smack across his shoulder as she mouthed, "Dewey," in complete and total embarrassment.

"Well…Trishy-Sue," Pops defended himself, "Beer Man has a point… The weeds are terrible this year."

"Friends…friends," Mayor Deradodo spoke loudly to quiet the unruly crowd.

He clutched his oversized belt buckle with both hands and rocked back on his heels.

"Not every bump in the night a ghost monster. And not every pee-stained sheet the work of a Tickle Monster. Tickle Monster gets ya…you know it! Tickle Monster gets ya…you die! Laugh so hard, you die… Any yas dead?"

The crowd looked around at each other like a bunch of kindergardening students after the teacher has asked, *"Who left mud on their shovels?"* A calmness filled the barning-barn as Mayor Deradodo paused and regained his composure. The large man gently slid on his big ole cowboy hat and wiggled it snug. It was so quiet I could hear Miss Poterspeel breathing like a geriatric banshee a few rows in front of me.

"Any yas heard laughing in the night?" The mayor asked the back of the barn room. "Any yas kids gone dead other than the Huggabees? Heard the girls drowned over yonder at Lake Sippo folks. Not from the Tickle Monster."

The mayor slowly grabbed his blazer from a chair on the stage and slid it on.

"One 'a them Huggabees sank from the weight of her back brace... Other girl's hair got caught in the back brace, and she drowned too... Huggabees died in water folks... Not in piss."

Bibs screamed, "Burn them sumbitch back braces!"

"Shoot 'em on sight!" Uncle Shty shouted.

"This bull bucks, ya here," Wheelchair Lesbo growled while stroking his Adams apple beard. "Best buckle up for a ride if ya want some of me!

"Back braces killin' Huggabees; grass ghosts hauntin' lawns; Tickle Monsters ticklin' toes... Whole damn town's going down the drain. I'll stand up out this wheelie chair if I has to!"

"Hunker down now folks! Hunker down," the mayor requested.

"Sometimes, we just pee the bed... Don't we?" he nodded to the old folks in the front row. "Let's not get worked up over a couple wet sheets. If I've told ya once, I've told ya a hundred times; better to have a pee-sheet problem than a poo-sheet problem!"

Ronny's father could always calm folks down during a tizzy. He just had a way with words.

"Let's all go home now, ya hear. Rest easy friends. Ain't no kids gettin' tickled in Big Rug tonight."

While exiting the barning barn, Pops pulled me under his arm with a smile and said, "Put honey by your bed, to wake up undead."

"Ah... Sir," Miss Poterspeel scolded from behind us, "The Huggabee girls are dead. This is hardly the time for shameful jokes."

As she walked away, Pops leaned down to me with a grin and whispered, "I know one person the Tickle Monster couldn't get to laugh... That dang Gray-Haired Goose!"

Today, all these years later, the Tickle Monster is still on Gus's mind. Gus owns a children's play fort business, appropriately named, Laugh Alive Forts. They're the highest quality playsets money can buy. They have shingles and windows and wooden floors and all kinds of good stuff. Each fort is custom built and comes with a jar of honey...to keep the Tickle Monster away.

I see Gus often these days. He's a regular at Boof and I's glove store. Building forts is hard work. Manual labor like that will wear down a set of work gloves. A talented man like Gus knows good tradesman apparel when he sees it, which is why he only wears Jesus Hands leather gloves! The mark of a true craftsman.

Gus is probably the most skilled handyman I've ever known. You name it; he can do it. Everything from skim-leveling a kitchen ditch before it puddles, to shaving a carpet stitch after it buckles; Gus is your guy.

One time, he fixed a hole in my shed by stuffing his t-shirt in it and securing both sides with scotch tape. That type of ingenuity takes decades of experience to develop. It's just like my grampy used to say,

"A boy grows into the gloves he's given." I guess Gus grew into his workin' man's gloves after all.

Even the *Big Rug Repository* has recognized Gus's exceptional fort building skills. One time they wrote an article about Laugh Alive Forts for their local business section. The newspaper fella interviewed Gus the same day he fixed my shed, so Gus was shirtless in the picture. He looked great though. One-hundred percent country hunk if I've ever seen one!

In the article, Gus was quoted as saying, "A lady-fella once told me, *'If you believe it, you can be it.'* I always believed one day I'd be a workin' man, and now, here I am…a man working."

Gus isn't the only person that's benefited from "believing" before "being." My Uncle Shty had a classmate who made a Halloween police uniform in seventh-grade home economics class. The boy sewed and stitched until every seam was just right. He loved his costume so much that he wore it all the time. Every day, he'd put on his police officer costume and walk around town with a pep in his step, proud of his sewing achievement.

After a while, he even started pretending to be a real man of the law. Folks around town kinda liked it though. He'd help old ladies cross the street and feed a few tree kids. He was a good boy. A little slow in the head, but harmless nonetheless.

Everyone just played along with his "man of the law" fantasies. They'd pat him on the head and say, "Keep up the good work young man," or "Nice job Mr. Deputy." Even Sheriff Beitzel entertained the young boy's delusions of authority by letting him ride in the squad car on the weekends.

Well, I'm here to tell you…that porridge-brained kid who walked around town in his self-made Halloween costume—believing he was a real man of the law—is none other than Shiffy! That's right… Mr. *"Ain't dat da trute"* himself…

And to this day, folks still pretend that Shiffy is a deputy. Ronny pays him a freakin' salary for heaven's sake. So that lady-fella who told Gus to, "believe and you can be," knew what she-he…or *he-she*, was talkin' 'bout… No doubt!

The face of a coward
is the back of their head
as they run from the battle.

— Yoderian proverb

BATTLE ON FIRST BOOB

The year Mitch rode off into the sunset—fly down—the Dust Fog Region had a winter blast that dumped twenty-five inches of snow in two days. All the schools across the region were closed for three weeks. The highs were in the single digits, and the lows were cold enough to crystalize your nose hairs. The boys and I got together to go sledding at First Boob Hill behind Jim Jim's Funeral Home, *"Your loss is our gain."* Best slogan in town, hands down!

On our way up First Boob, the boys and I were ambushed with snowballs. The white orbs of ice shot through the air from multiple directions. They were coming hard and coming fast. Like Jet and Queenie running down that gravel alleyway on the day they tried to eat us boys alive.

"Take cover," Larry yelled, covering his head from the onslaught of snowballs.

"Behind the trees," Dale commanded while hip-sliding behind an oak tree's trunk.

"My eye," Ronny howled.

Thankfully, Ronny didn't actually take a snowball to the eye. Captain Klutz swung his arms a little too aggressively while running and smacked himself in the face. Honestly...I don't know how that boy is still alive... The Deradodo Clumsy Curse keeps trying, but Ronny keeps surviving.

We dove behind trees as if atomic bombs were dropping from the sky. I jumped head first off the sledding path and quickly scooted up behind a tree for shelter.

"Ouch," Ronny cried out again. "My elbow hit a rock," he moaned, rolling around in the snow.

My heart raced as snowballs exploded around me. Who was attacking us? What kind of scoundrel would display such aggression on a snow day?

I squeezed my eyes shut, attempting to calm my nerves and make sense of the situation, but the cries of my fallen comrades tormented my mind. A deep breath of cold air filled my lungs as my eyes opened to a winter wonder war zone. I started searching for my hat, that had fallen off in the panic, when I heard the voice of an all too familiar enemy...the Ferry Flowers of Stoolmist!

"I thought skunk weasels were nocturnal creatures," Preston called out from the top of the hill like a little butt-weed.

"Your mom's a nocturnal creature," Dale responded awesomely!

I peeked around the tree shielding me and saw all four Ferry Flowers standing at the top of First Boob, hurling snowballs in our direction. They had the high-ground. They had the ammunition. They had us trapped and divided, compromising our ability to organize a proper defense. There was no escape... And there was no surrender.

My grampy used to say, "If you can't run away, then you gotta face the day." And so, with no choice but for us boys to shelter in place and face the day, The Battle on First Boob began!

"Gather ammunition!" Larry shouted, as giggling children sledded past us, unaware of the ensuing war.

Just as soon as we started packing snowballs, Ronny—in a moment of bravery—ran out from behind his shelter and screamed with all his might, "Skunk weasels unite!"

A rallying cry none of us had ever used before, but sounded incredible in the moment. Even today, it still gives me goosebumps just thinkin' 'bout it... Sometimes, when Brekanny and I are in the heat of passion, I'll inadvertently yell out, "Skunk weasels unite!" Brekanny says it's a total mood killer. But, during The Battle on First Boob, it definitely got us boys in the mood!

Unfortunately, as soon as Ronny ran out onto the sledding path and shouted the rallying cry, his legs were taken out from underneath him by a tiny-tike on a silver disc sled cruisin' down the hill. That little kid was going faster than a coon-cat on a mud-rat when she hit Ronny's legs. And she just kept cruisin' down the hill like nothin' happened.

Ronny smacked his forehead pretty hard on the compacted snow, knocking him unconscious. He could've been seriously injured if not for his stocking cap with the little ball on top.

Now, that day, out there on First Boob, Ronny's little saying, "If used by Truce, it must have a use," actually made sense. Because that stocking cap probably saved him from permanently needing to wear a pair of Big Ups.

Captain Klutz slowly slid down the hill, face first, and motionless, leaving a pitter patter of red blood in the white snow; like a little trail leading to his whereabouts. All that remained was his stocking cap sitting in the middle of the path, with an occasional sledder zipping over it. The Battle on First Boob had claimed its first victim. And to my chagrin, I knew he wouldn't be the last.

I watched Ronny slide all the way down to the bottom of the hill where Brant was building a snow fort, completely unaware of the battle the boys and I were in just fifty yards uphill.

"Where's Cat Piss, Mitch?" Fat Neck Oliver yelled while the rest of the Ferry Flowers launched snowballs. "Fly-Downs afraid of snow or something?"

Preston stood tall at the top of the hill and arrogantly announced, "Surrender! And we'll let you sled on Third Boob."

The nerve of that guy… "The Boobs"—the name folks use when referring to the three large hills bordering Big Rug and Owdina National Park—are in Big Rug! So, no Stoolmist sally sack fart fanning skin flap was going to tell us where we could, and couldn't, sled in our own town!

And, Third Boob sucked! The hill was for kindergardeners and your occasional elderly sledder. It was amateur hour… The mere suggestion that we would go sledding on Third Boob was insulting.

Uncle Shty and Cornbread used to sit in lawn chairs at the top of Third Boob and try to sell mowers to the parents chaperoning their children. Coach typically joined too. But he went so he could practice boot-sliding down the hill in his big city boxer brief shorts.

"Cold don't bother me," Coach would say, puffing out his chest with his legs glowing red from snow-burn. "That's how they s'pposed to be," he'd yell when folks called attention to his frost-bitten thighs.

"These are Big Rug's Boobs," I yelled at the Ferry Flowers from behind my tree. "We own The Boobs, and you chunker-bunkers know it. So, go push a plow, you no good rabble rousers."

One time, Redman called us boys a bunch of rabble rousers while chasing us off his farm. I'd been saving those words for a special occasion…and The Battle on First Boob was that occasion!

But then…as if the words I spoke unleashed some sorta' geriatric demon from within my soul, the spirit of Redman took over my body, and I continued screaming uncontrollably up the hill.

"Ye dang nasty trolleys… *Ye nasty trolleys, I say*! Damn dirty bastard birds. Dirt pigeons, I say… Dirt pigeons!"

In my peripheral, I saw a group of betties laughing at my strange outburst. It was super embarrassing… But before I could even blush, a snowball struck me square in the chest.

"Skunk weasels are junk weasels," Stinkin' Lincoln yelled while throwing another snowball at me.

"Big Rugians can't farm," Oliver added with his fat neck.

"You can't farm," I replied.

"You don't know jack squat!" Oliver erupted.

The exchange of repeating insults went on for several minutes while Larry and I quickly packed snowballs for our attack.

"Softball size, Larry…" I insisted. "Softball size."

Our snowballs needed to pack a punch. This was no time for half-assing it on packing snow. We needed premium ammunition if we were to survive.

I looked across the sledding path at Gus to check on his snowball supply and saw him doing the strangest thing. He was laying sideways with his snow pants pulled down around his knees—struggling to pull his leather gloves off with his teeth—while attempting to pee on a pile of snowballs.

"Pissy balls…" he giggled.

The minutes seemed like hours as I watched innocent children laughing in delight, sledding down the hill, giving the war zone an uncomfortable aura. Like when you enter a funhouse at the fair and its uncomfortably apparent that the carny gentleman "working in" the funhouse is also "living in" the funhouse…

"Shields up," Larry ordered while lifting his sled.

I looked over at Chad, curled up behind a tree, trying to control his breathing. His eyes were closed as he grappled with the reality of what lie ahead. He opened his eyes and looked at me, and I at him, finding strength in one another to do what must be done. To fight; and not to run.

"Preston," Larry called out like a total stud muffin. "Tenth grade... Honey Farm Fair... Dead Tree Cemetery..."

"What about it...you no good skunk-junk," Preston's raging voice rumbled through the forest.

"You ran," Larry roared. "I climbed..."

He lowered his head and kissed the small gold cross hanging from his neck. We watched as he grabbed a few snowballs and nodded at us boys.

"Let 'em rip," he bellowed, like a Greek God shouting down from the heavens above.

And with those three words, us boys rushed to the center of the sledding path during The Battle on First Boob and heaved snowballs in defense of The Boobs, the town of Big Rug, and all those in the Dustfog Region who's ever had to endure crossing paths with a yuppie-guppy from Stoolmist.

Immediately, I saw Preston take a snowball right to the kisser, causing him to fall back in retreat. We unloaded without caution as the adrenaline pumped power behind every throw.

"Pissy balls firing," Gus hollered.

"Butt-mist sucks!" Dale taunted while running from one tree to another, throwing snowballs in between.

Once our ammunition was depleted, we lowered our sleds to assess the damage. The Ferry Flowers fled immediately after Preston's face got blasted by Larry's first throw. Preston may have been tough, but a softball size snowball to the mush will bend the knee of any man.

Regretfully—being unaware of how quickly we'd defeated the Ferry Flowers—we kept firing rounds of ammunition in the moment of battle, pulling several innocent victims into our wrath. Women, children, even a small dog, had the misfortune of being collateral damage in what I can only assume was the most terrifying moment of their lives.

I looked up and saw Andrea Huggabee batting snow out of her sister Haley's hair. Both girls were clearly upset from witnessing the most horrific battle in the history of the Dustfog Region.

I'm sure the sisters were thankful to be alive though. The battlefield is an unforgiving place. The good Lord was looking out for the Huggabees during The Battle on First Boob… No doubt!

However, at that moment, I was shocked to see the Huggabees. A few weeks earlier, Cousin Fannie told me they died in a sledding accident up at Devil's Dip on Second Boob. The whole town was upset. Mr. McGilbert and Preacher Jepp led a prayer vigil at The Manhole for the town to mourn the loss of the Huggabees. Mama was in tears for a week. She baked a casserole for heaven's sake!

Fannie said the Huggabees were double-cruisin' on one of those old-timey toboggans when their scarves got caught on a branch and popped their heads off.

Heck, Gus even talked to the guy who thought he found the Huggabee's scarves dangling from a branch. Seemed reasonable at the time to assume the sisters were decapitated. If you find a scarf laying around a dangerous sledding trail, and no one's around, what exactly are you supposed to assume happened?

"Sorry Haley," Larry hollered up the hill.

"You jerks!" she screeched, red in the face while helping Andrea get snow off her shoulder.

"Wait… Haley?" Chad called out. "Andrea…? Is that you up there…? Aren't you two dead or something?"

The girls stopped batting snow out of their hair and glared with disgust at Chad.

"You're all a bunch of morons," Haley whined, picking up snow and throwing it downhill as a gust of wind blew the snow powder back into her face.

"I thought they were dead too," Gus confessed. "At least, that's what Tuck told me.

I quickly defended myself, "They are dead! They were decapitated up at Devils-Dip."

"Tuck's right," Dale said. "The Huggabees aren't on the school roster anymore. I've seen them at school, but I figured they were ghosts. To be sure, I've been throwing erasers at them during class. Cause stuff goes through ghosts… You know?"

"Did the erasers go through them?" Larry asked.

"Nope… They've been bouncing off. Even when it's been a head shot… But, the erasers kinda have a sparkly look to them, so they might be magic erasers? The kind that can magically hit a ghost… I'm not totally positive though…

So, to be safe, lately when I see the Huggabees in the hallway, I throw an eraser at them, and then scream and run away."

"Weird," Larry pondered, rubbing his chin. "But smart… That's what I'd do."

Gus stepped forward, pushing us out of the way.

"Hold on, hold on," he said while packing a snowball. "I know exactly what to do."

Gus confidently placed a fresh jerky stick into his mouth and pulled his gloves tight. He cocked his arm back and threw a snowball up the hill at the Huggabees as they were walking away, nailing Haley right between her shoulder blades. The snowball exploded on her puffy pink jacket with a *thud*.

"Beef cigar," Gus celebrated.

Haley swung around and shouted, "What the heck is wrong with you idiots?"

The boys and I watched quietly, waiting for something "ghostly" to happen...

"Nope," Gus concluded, patting the snow off his gloves. "Those ain't no ghosts. Snowballs go through ghosts," he said chomping on a jerky stick. "That's a fact!"

As we turned and started walking down the hill, Larry shared, "I heard their mother got remarried or something? To the fella workin' the register over at Stuff & Stuff's Nice Things. Heard it at Mitch's birthday party from someone, I think? I don't know? Those hot-tarties had my ears ringing."

"Ha," Gus replied. "Heard their mom remarried, did ya? You can't believe every little thing you hear around town, Larry. That's how rumors get started!"

At the bottom of First Boob, we found a conscious Ronny tending to his wounds while watching Brant put the finishing touches on a snow fort. I'll never forget the moment I crawled in that snow fort and saw a fully-functioning oven made of snow in the corner.

I swear on a pair of red silk over the shoulder boulder holders that Brant had a fire in that oven made of snow! And, inside was a freshly baked cheese pizza! I saw it with my own eyes… It wasn't delivery. It was SnowGiorno; a name I came up with—on the spot—and still own the intellectual rights to.

I might not be the sharpest tool in the shed, but I know a good business opportunity when I see one. And SnowGiorno was that opportunity… Even more than Tramp-O-Jeans or the Sluttie.

How is it possible to have a fire in snow, you might ask… Well, Mr. Stoltzer theorized that the fire in the oven would melt the snow while, simultaneously, the wind on First Boob would swirl so fast, and so cold, that it would refreeze the snow before it lost its structural integrity. To this day, the science community has yet to explain this amazing contemporaneous melting and freezing of snow.

To add legitimacy to this scientific phenomenon, I combined the words "freeze" and "melting" to coin the term "meltzing." Meltzing is a real thing… My wife says it's something called a verb.

Meltzing would have been the "secret formula" to an oven-fresh SnowGiorno. Our competitive advantage in the pizza market place.

But, just as soon as the boys and I realized we were witnessing a scientific breakthrough—and an incredible restaurant opportunity—Shiffy and the sheriff showed up to ruin our day.

"Got a call from Miss Poterspeel a bunch of boys startin' fires," the sheriff cursed while stumbling toward us through the snow. "That a fort…? Ya'll got a permit to build?"

"Wait a darn sec…" he paused and perked up. "Do I smell pizza? Shiffy, crawl on in there n' grab that pizza for evidence."

Shiffy ungracefully squeezed halfway into the fort and grabbed the last slice of pizza out of the oven made of snow.

"This fresh pizza?" the sheriff mumbled with his mouth full. "Sure do taste fresh."

"It's SnowGiorno," I whispered in sorrow.

"Can I get a bite of that," Gus pleaded. "I only got one slice, and it was mostly crust."

"You a lawman?" the sheriff barked. "This look like fun to you? This work son!" he scolded with a pizza slice in one hand and a sled in the other. "And... I ain't sleddin' for fun neither... I gotta test the hills for safety. Part of the job! I put my life at risk every day, in a lotta different ways.

"You boys gonna hurt someone with that dang fire. Y'all know Big Rug got high levels of gasoline in the snow. Whole town could burn 'cause 'a y'all boys," he reprimanded, while waving the crust of the pizza at us.

"And who likes plain cheese pizza anyway? Put some dang meats on it why don't ya! Toppins dang it... Toppins!"

Shiffy popped his head out of the fort and screamed, "Ain't dat da trute," at the top of his lungs.

"Shut it Shiffy," the sheriff shouted. "Why ya gotta be screamin' dang it? I knows the pizza toppins. You don't know toppins! Did you work in a pizza place when you was a kid? *No!* I did... For almost half a day before quitting. I knows the toppins!"

"If y'all dang boys had somethin' proper, like a little bit 'a sausage on it, I might let y'all go. But no! Y'all gotta go and do somethin' silly like not puttin' no toppins on no pizza. Lucky I don't put y'all in cuffs," he ranted while taking another bite. "No toppins on no pizza."

"Ain't dat da trute," Shiffy yelled again, swinging his arms and accidently knocking the pizza from the sheriff's hand.

"Ding dang doggone it, Shiffy. That's the crust... Da crust dang it," the sheriff shrieked like a twelve-year-old girl. "You know I had a light breakfast! Now the crust in the gas snow. I can't eat no gas snow pizza crust... Acid reflux Shiffy... *Acid reflux,*" he gripped while stomping around in the snow.

Shiffy's hat blew off as the wind on First Boob began to swirl. The dark clouds of a cold front approached from the north while the fire in the fort growled with each gust.

I lifted my gloved hands to shield my face from the chilled air drying my eyes and burning my cheeks. The dust-like snow crystals spiraling through the flurries felt like frozen needles as they pricked against my skin.

"Ding dang doggone it, Shiffy," Sheriff Beitzel complained while kicking the snow-covered crust.

It was a good kick by the sheriff. He even kinda pointed one of his fingers in the air like he was kicking a field goal or something… There was a ring of keys on his hip that jingled as the fat man took a few steps in his approach for the kick. Unfortunately, he slipped and took a nose dive into the snow fort.

"Help me! Snow in my britches. Snow in my britches Shiffy," he squealed like a barn-hog while Shiffy struggled to lift him.

"Gettin' the frosty bites…" he moaned while untucking his shirt and fanning out the snow that snuck in through his collar. "Burnin' me Shiffy… Oh Lord…snow burnin' me. Went down my shirt, Shiffy! It's burnin'!"

Shiffy screamed, "Stop, drop, roll," as he tackled Sheriff Beitzel from behind, belly flopping the fat man back into the fort.

"Ding dang doggone it, Shiffy," the sheriff yelped as they wrestled around. "I ain't on fire damn it! Burnin' from the cold… Burnin' from the cold, Shiffy!"

As we watched the two men flailing in the snow, I noticed Brant was missing. Which wasn't exactly unusual for that kid. But, watching Shiffy and the sheriff wrestling in the snow was hysterical. Brant wouldn't miss a moment like that.

While the lawmen struggled to get themselves out of the snow, the boys and I snuck away and searched for Brant. Eventually we made our way to his house where we found him racing down the stairs with his camera around his neck. He leapt off a step and soared over YoUber, who was napping at the landing of the staircase where the warm sun shines through the windows.

His feet hit the floor with a thud as he swung a backpack over his shoulder. The cold front rolling in from the north had engulfed us. The heavy clouds darkened the sky as snowflakes raced through the bitter wind. The cold was unforgiving; and so was Brant.

The boys and I stood there, in the chill of the storm, watching Brant tear through the house. He grabbed two Yoo-hoo's, a *Boy's Life Magazine*, a pack of Double-Bubble chewing gum, and ran out the door; stopping in the tumbling snow to turn back at us boys.

"Fellas," he shouted through the storm, "I'm finding a new home."

And just like that, Brant disappeared into the blizzard.

His parents never made a fuss about his disappearance, so I knew he was okay, but he never returned nonetheless. Not for the Honey Farm Fair in May. Not for Walk on Water Wednesday Worship in July. Not for Old Mold on the Lake, Fall Fest in Mumper, or the Lumberers of the Valley tournament. Not for Beef Jerky While You Worky Day at school or to listen to the sweet spoonings of Bozo Goober. Not for nothin'. Brant was just…gone.

Find comfort in thy Lord;
for in him is home.

— *Yoderian proverb*

ANYWHERE THAT'S HOME

My mother used to joke that you could drop Brant off in the middle of nowhere, with nothing but socks soaked in eggs, and in a week, he'd have food, shelter, and enough time to start a new hobby. He was a resourceful boy if I've ever met one. On Grampy and Granny's grave, I once watched the kid tie a chuckle-buckle-knot outta jumper cables... Nuff said!

On most days, Brant was roaming around town taking photographs. Never of people though. Only of objects. The Ormish strictly forbid being photographed or photographing others. His favorite thing to shoot was the, "Smoke of a campfire swirling in the backdrop of a beautiful world," as he used to say.

His thirty-two hair locks would graze across his brown shoulders in the summertime as he walked around the forest barefoot, snapping pictures of this and that. For an outdoors kinda guy, he never smelled as bad as you'd think. He'd bathe in streams, use the sand to exfoliate his skin, and rub smell-good plants on himself.

"I'm living our intentional design," he'd tell us boys while rubbing Rosemary under his armpits. "Like my Ormish ancestors did. It's a spiritual thing."

Personally, I was never impressed with Brant's rejection of hygiene, or spiritual path, or whatever he wanted to call it. I respected it, but not washing your hair? Not wearing deodorant? I'm not interested... Call me when there's a spiritual path where you don't have to floss! That's a belief system I can commit to.

Brant took after his mother, Tulip, when it came to his brains. Tulip is a dark-haired, olive-skinned, tiny lady with a mouth that goes a mile a minute. Most Ormish folks are reserved and mild mannered, but Tulip doesn't have time for no nonsense!

"Be bold and brief," she says when patients visit her at the Big Rug Feel Good Clinic.

My mother adores Tulip. She has since the day she met her. When Boof and I were kids, she'd use Tulip as an example of accomplishing anything we put our minds to.

"Just look at Brant's mother, Tulip," she'd say. "An Ormish girl, grown up to be a doctor. I pray the two of you grow up to be a woman like that someday."

Having your mom repeatedly tell you that she hopes you grow up to be a "woman like that," can mess with the head of a young boy. In the fourth grade when Mrs. Boil asked the class to share what we wanted to be when we grow up, I stood up confidently and said, "I wanna be a lady like Brant's mom."

Everyone laughed... Even Mrs. Boil laughed at me.

I was so embarrassed. I felt like I'd stepped in a duck-log while dancin' in my church shoes. Thankfully, Gus was sneaking a bite of brisket hidden in his pencil holder and choked on it when he started laughing. It served as a great distraction from my humiliation.

And, that was the day Ronny mistakenly told the class that he wanted to be a "gynecologist" instead of a "geologist." So, no one really remembered the whole, "I want to be a lady thing."

Which is fortunate, because years later in high school, I mistakenly grabbed my mom's cherry-red lipstick instead of her cherry chap stick. I walked around all day with lipstick on and had no idea. Can you imagine how embarrassing that would've been if folks remembered the, "I want to be a lady" thing back in the fourth grade?

And, like many high school boys, I was going through a pierced-ear phase. By the sweet grace of God, I chose to wear my fire hydrant red sparkplug earring that Brant made me for my tenth birthday… So at least my lipstick and earring matched. Otherwise, I would've looked like a fool!

Sometimes, in the middle of the night, I'll wake up in a cold sweat while dreaming about the tragic events that took place during The Battle on First Boob. There's no doubt that us boys—and many of the innocent bystanders—lost a piece of our innocence on that day. Although much was gained with our victory over the Ferry Flowers, much was lost.

A few years after Brant ran away, I learned that he'd been living in the Owdina National Park ranger stations. Earl and Tulip saw him every week, but never told anyone for fear that Earl could lose his park ranger job for letting a non-ranger stay in a station overnight.

Brant wondered between ranger stations—depending on which area of the park Earl was working that month—and did all the things that Brant loved to do. He explored nature, built campfires, and took photos of the smoke swirling in the backdrop of a beautiful world.

As an adult, Brant has written and published dozens of articles for multiple publications, on topics ranging from the weather patterns of deep valley terrains, to holistic medicine for the world traveler. But it's the topic of campfires that he's written about the most. His National Geographic article, "The Art of the Flame," detailed twenty-six different ways to build a campfire, each with their own name, and each with their own intended purpose. The Boy Scouts even made "The Art of the Flame" an optional read to earn an Advanced Fire Safety merit badge.

However, nothing Brant has written compares to his photographs. All who lay eyes on his work are astonished by his ability to capture the elegant billowing of smoke as it rolls off the flames of a campfire. The imagery of little red embers tracing through the shadows of bending purple smoke is incredibly beautiful when Brant's technique is used. A technique held secret by Brant, and Brant alone. A technique that has earned him fame and fortune. In the same way that *meltzing* would have done for me, in my never pursued SnowGiorno pizza restaurant.

Brant's most valuable piece to date is a photograph titled *Cold Curves*, taken in the Marble Caves of the Patagonia Andes. Only accessible by boat, the peninsula of solid marble hovers above General Carrera Lake in the shared waters of Argentina and Chile.

Cold Curves is a colorful image of the gray smoke of a water-floating-fire with yellow-red embers flashing against swirling blues of marble. The smoke looks as if it's the silhouette of a curvaceous young woman. Art enthusiasts say that Brant caught mother nature in a photo, and she's as beautiful as imagined.

The work of art sold at an auction for a whopping eight-hundred-thousand dollars. At one cent for five spark plugs, Brant would've been able to buy four-hundred-million old spark plugs from Uncle

Shty back when we were kids. In the words of my beautiful mother, and on behalf of all the women across the Dustfog Region walking around with stretched earlobes from Brant's sparkplug earrings, "That's the price you pay for fashion!"

But fame and fortune never interested Brant. Even today, it seems he still doesn't care for the more glamorous offerings of his talents. The majority of his earnings are donated to the National Park Services. He has never made a public appearance, never sat for an interview, and there are no known images of Brant.

One time, his photographs were exhibited at the National Gallery of Art in Washington D.C. for all to enjoy. I wasn't able to attend, but Ronny went, and he showed me the pamphlet they gave guests as they entered the museum. The exhibit looked fancy. The type 'a thing you'd buy breath mints for.

In the Grand Hall of the museum, there hung a banner displaying a short bio of Brant—without an accompanying portrait—that described him as, "The ghost of photography." But to us boys still living in town, hoping for our long-lost friend to one day return, it could've just as easily read "The ghost of Big Rug."

When Brekanny turned forty, I took a six-day trip out west to pick up a truck for her birthday. Things sure are different when you travel outta town. Most days, it felt like I didn't recognize the world, or the world didn't recognize me. To be honest, on most days…I just felt really alone. Like a stranger that no one cared to befriend.

Heck…I didn't meet a single pinky-pointer livin' up to their potential while I was traveling. Gaywads are supposed to be the trend setters of their communities. But clearly, big city feather-foots don't take that responsibility as seriously as the homos in my neck of the woods. I didn't meet a single limp wrist who shook my hand with sass!

The second morning of the bus trip, I woke to the early-morning commotion of passengers shifting through their bags. As the old Greyhound bus stopped at a cross street, the brakes squealed like a futuristic mechanical rooster crowing at the sunrise.

I lifted my head from the morning-chilled window and saw the most glorious display of colors reflecting off a wall of glass spanning the front of a small coffee shop. Oranges blended to blues, as rays of light glowed in the pass throughs, like a watercolor painting stretching from horizon to horizon. And below the brilliant sky stood a mountain within mountains holding blankets of snow crowned upon her peaks.

It was like opening my eyes inside of a real-life Pucker Loaf painting. Half asleep and half awake, I could see the reflection of the mountain in the coffee shop windows. I was completely and totally consumed by the image set before me. If Mrs. Yoder's Mountain had a lovely younger sister, I was surely gazing upon the majesty of her beauty.

The brain-fog of my semi-sleep paralysis slowly cleared as my eyes focused through the reflections of the coffee shop windows. Sitting inside the café, I saw an olive-skinned man drinking coffee and writing in a journal. His long hair, matted into locks, reached down just below his shoulders and was as black as his wiry beard.

While my bus pulled away from the hidden town in heaven, the olive-skinned man looked up, and our eyes met for but a moment. I can say with unequivocal certainty, that I saw the eyes of the boy I once knew.

All these years later, I still wonder if Brant recognized me, the way I recognized him. If he saw the eyes of a long-lost friend peering at him through an old bus window as it pulled away into a new day's dawn. Sometimes, I tell myself I could hear someone yelling, "Yawp," from outside the bus as we pulled away. But deep down, I know it was just an old man tooting in the back of the bus.

After picking up my wife's truck, I traveled through the little town in the mountains once more. I stopped for lunch at the coffee shop and inquired about the man I saw; but no one had anything to share.

I was hoping someone would say, *"Oh ya, that's so-n'-so, he lives down by this-n'-that. He comes in here every now-n'-again."*

But to the coffee shop gal's, he was nothing more than a face they'd never seen… And for me, unfortunately, the man I'd hoped to find was nothing more than a reflection in the windows of a mountain town café. The ghost of a friend I longed to see again.

In the cool fall evenings of Big Rug, Brekanny and I will sit around a campfire with the kids and roast yoke berries. Brekanny enjoys gazing at our children as they watch their berries bubble in the fire, but my eyes always drift to the smoke swirling in the backdrop of a beautiful world.

As the evenings grow quiet, I'm often left alone for a brief moment as my wife readies the children for bed. Sometimes, when the moon is round and ripe, flooding the valley with silver light, casting shadows into the darkness of night, I can see an image of the friends I've lost in my mind's eye.

An image of The Navy Blue swimming in the tropical paradise of New Jersey. Mitch riding into the sunset…fly down. And an image of Brant, hidden in the trees that are hidden in the mountains that are hidden in the clouds, wisping through an endless sky, like the billowing smoke of a campfire. And on those nights, accompanied only by the gazing moon, I know my friends have found a home to call their own, wherever that home may be.

Recently, a Canadian journalist passed through town while on assignment. He was a young fella with curly black hair wearing eyeglasses that darkened as he stepped into the sunlight. Miss Poterspeel—having just celebrated her ninety-eighth birthday— immediately accused the journalist of witchcraft upon seeing his glasses "magically" change colors.

So, Sheriff Beitzel detained the journalist for the minimum "two-hour witchcraft accusation holding period," while Preacher Jepp inspected the magic glasses. He determined fairly quickly that the journalist was not a purveyor of witchcraft. But the Gray-Haired Goose was convinced.

"He's one of them Magics," she insisted. "They live in the sewers of the city and spread their sex diseases and diabetes."

Most folks round these parts remember the journalist's arrival pretty well, because Miss Poterspeel died—peacefully from old age, I might add—the next evening. She was found dead in her bed with a note in her hand that read, "If I die tonight, it's because of that pervert man-witch with the devil glasses."

The young journalist told us he was documenting life in the forgotten towns in-between cities. Although his introduction to the town of Big Rug was less than ideal, he still wrote a beautiful paragraph in an article titled, "A Path Less Traveled."

What the journalist wrote about our town was so beautiful, the volunteers down at the Ferris Wheel Chapel stenciled it—word-for-word—on the side of the Big Rug Town Hall and Drive-Through Deli. Took them all summer to get every word spelled just right.

Pucker Loaf even painted a few sunflowers growing out of rusty hubcaps around the edges. Very classy…

The excerpt reads:

> *"Skunks are a problem in the town of Big Rug. A common morning routine for Big Rugians is to spritz oneself with vinegar in anticipation of being sprayed by a skunk. The smell of vinegar is believed to overpower the scent of the skunk. Whether you're smelling skunk or smelling vinegar, the town of Big Rug has an odor that no place on Earth can match."*

I agree with every word that kind journalist wrote about the town I love. To this day, it still fills my heart with pride when I hear someone joyfully recite this beautiful paragraph at a wedding, sporting event, or special occasion.

There's no place on Earth that can match the town of Big Rug! It's just like my grampy used to say, "If it's one-of-a-kind, I want it for mine." And although some have left this lovely community, never to return, for me…there's no place I'd rather call home.

Nuff said.

If this book brought you joy,

please, offer that joy to another.

Share that you've read,

The Boys of Big Rug.

ABOUT THE AUTHOR

———

T.J. Morgan is an American author, artist, and—most importantly—a husband and father to a family he adores. Born and raised in North Canton, OH, he found his way to Edmond, OK where he attended the University of Central Oklahoma and earned his BBA and MBA. He is passionate about creating engaging stories that offer a complete experience of visual and emotional entertainment.

An avid supporter of art, music, and the outdoors, T.J. finds inspiration in the everyday balance of life. He encourages others to live lives of gratitude and to release that joy into the world. T.J. has been blessed to offer his talents through his novels and children's picture books; available where books are sold.